I, Lloyd Stollman

I, Lloyd Stollman

Rob Sullivan

Black Heron Press
Post Office Box 614
Anacortes, Washington 98221
www.blackheronpress.com

ISBN (print): 978-1-936364-40-4
ISBN (ebook): 978-1-936364-41-1

Cover and art design by Bryan Sears

Black Heron Press
Post Office Box 614
Anacortes, Washington
www.blackheronpress.com

For Casey, Quinn and Ezra

1

I only started to feel right when I put on my first disguise. Before that, I had been a half-person, a shadow, a ghost, a nonentity, anonymous, dead. But once I put that disguise on, I felt like I fit in my own body, that I belonged, that I was part of society, like I had a place, like I was somebody. All I had to do was walk down the street with my moustache on and that nice big Stetson, the cowboy boots and the blue jeans and I felt like I had arrived.

Not that anyone did anything or reacted in some kind of blatantly odd manner, pointing at me or whispering about me or something like that. It was the very fact that none of these things happened that made me feel like I was a success. I had passed, no one noticed, no one said anything, no one did anything, no one even turned or nodded or said hello.

It was such a revelation. It was such a relief. Not to have to be myself. Not to have to walk down the street with my own face on. By allowing myself to cover myself, I had been revealed. By allowing myself to cover myself, I had become myself. The mustache, the hat, the blue jeans and the cowboy boots, they had fused around me, holding me together in their disguise while I walked the streets of my neighborhood in the West Adams area of L.A.

Yes, I live in that city. The one everyone loves to hate and the one everyone hates to love. The city of Watts and the city of the Hollywood sign. The city of the crazies in Venice and the city of the puffed-up and preposterous in Beverly Hills. The city of fame and the town of broken dreams. The city of the Dodgers and the city of the Lakers, the city of traffic congestion and the city of surfers, their boards running down the sides of waves with their bizarre swerving liquid patterns. I've been here all my life and know no other city. Oh, I've visited San Francisco and New York, and I've even been to Paris and London and Rome on one of those crazy student tours where you do thirteen cities in eight days, just so you can say you've been there. But this is the only place I really know and I've always been a stranger here.

Until that day I went out in disguise. That's when everything changed. That's when the whole world opened up.

At first I didn't kill anybody. My mind wasn't even headed toward crime, it didn't even occur to me. Just walking out in public in a disguise felt wild enough. Why should I commit a crime when I could walk down the street in a cowboy suit? I was happy just not being who I was, a lonely guy with no true friends who pretty much had wasted his life. Well, maybe wasted is too strong a word, maybe just diddled it away would be better, though that sounds pretty awful too. But it was true. All I had done was graduate from Long Beach State and then spend twenty-five years working at the Culver City DMV in one of those little cubicles. I was the one who took the pictures. I must have snapped a million photos in the twenty-five years I was there. I've seen so many faces, fat ones and thin ones, old ones and young ones, freckled faces of kids who still had that upbeat spirit of thinking they were going to conquer the world, and worn-out faces of old guys whose disappointment with their lives was carved into their faces. Some of the faces were mysterious and wonderful and some were bland as hell. I had one lady die on me right as she was getting her photo snapped. Boom, she just keels over and that was that. Heart attack is what they said. In a weird way, I felt a little responsible, like maybe by taking that picture I had triggered the attack. But that's crazy, really. And one thing

I'm not is crazy.

The first time I wore a disguise I just walked down to the CVS on Western and bought me some shampoo. Real simple, nothing fancy. When I spoke to the clerk, I used a little bit of a drawl like I was a high plains drifter, just like Clint Eastwood in the movie of the same name. A man of few words, the real cowboy doesn't need to say much. His stance says it all, his composure and his diction, the spare way he uses words, the squint in his eye. No one said anything back to me except the clerk with the usual pleasantries. They all thought I was a cowboy, if they thought anything at all. One thing about being a customer, as long as you are basically well behaved and have the money to pay for the goods you can be whomsoever you want to be. All they care about is cash on the barrel.

You know, on second thought, maybe I didn't diddle my life away. I mean I did graduate from college and I did keep that job at the DMV all those years. So at least I wasn't a burden on society. I was a pretty good uncle, I think, to my niece and nephew. Well, at least when they were little. Later on, we kind of stopped communicating, though I always remembered their birthdays and sent them a card with some cash tucked inside, usually fifty bucks, but once in a while a hundred. They'd always call me then and say thanks and we'd exchange a few remarks but it wasn't much more than that. And now that I've killed all these people, you can't really say my life didn't amount to much, even if some might think I have a negative rather than a positive balance in my moral bank account.

Walking down Venice Boulevard after that adventure at the pharmacy, buying shampoo in my cowboy suit, I was just—I don't know—glowing. It felt so great to have been someone else, even if only for a fleeting moment. And to be a cowboy! I mean I'm old enough to have grown up in the heyday of the Westerns,

The Magnificent Seven with Steve McQueen and Yul Brynner and Charles Bronson and James Coburn, or *The Horse Soldiers* with John Wayne and William Holden, or those great old Western TV shows from the 50s and 60s like *Have Gun Will Travel* with Richard Boone, or *Wanted: Dead or Alive* with McQueen back before he became such a big movie star, or *The Rifleman* with Chuck Connors or *Maverick* with James Garner. I watched all of those shows when I was a little kid and that's kind of how I learned to be a man. By watching these guys. They were tough and lean and they didn't take crap from no one and man, were they quick on the draw, they could shoot you down dead before you even knew what was coming.

So walking back home with the shampoo in a plastic bag and me in my cowboy gear really made me feel good. I felt like I was shining, that everyone could see this light coming out of me and filling up the streets and the sky with this Tombstone glow. The only thing missing was a gun.

When I got back to my apartment, I looked in the mirror and grinned. Shit, I didn't just grin: let's be honest here: I cried out loud and whooped and hollered with laughter and joy and glee, taking off my hat and whipping it across my knee. Giddy with having fooled everyone, I got out a beer and celebrated. Man, that tasted good! That was probably the most delicious drink I have ever had in my entire life, that soothing quality as it laced its way down my throat and landed in my guts with a nice little splash, like I'd just inhaled a streak of a rainbow or something. After finishing off the beer in two or three gulps, I slowly took off my boots and my blue jeans and put them carefully away. Next was the shirt which I hung back up in the closet. The last thing to go was the hat. That I put on top of the dresser so it sort of crowned it just as the Stetson crowned my head when I wore it.

When I lay down in bed that night to go to sleep, everything felt cozy and warm. It was so nice. I don't think I'd felt this way since I was a kid. I stared up at the ceiling, thinking about the day's adventure. I'd been a cowboy! Honest to god, I had been a cowboy. What a magnificent thing that was. And it hadn't just been me walking down Venice to the pharmacy. It was me and Steve McQueen and me and Charles Bronson and me and John Wayne and me and Richard Boone and me and all of them, they had been walking right by my side. All of us gunmen striding down the road together like a gang or a posse. All of us outlaws together. Sure as shit, no one was going to mess with us. Otherwise, they'd be dead, and pronto. Can you imagine what it felt like to walk with those hombres down the street? Probably not, as it's pretty damn hard for me to imagine it and I'm the one who did it.

I went to sleep grinning. And that's no metaphor or literary conceit or whatever they call it these days. I mean that I was actually smiling as I drifted off to sleep. I had had such a great day. And I couldn't wait for the next one. For what kind of adventure would the next day bring, given that this one had been so brilliant and so beautiful?

2

The next morning I had no idea what to do. What could top what I had done the day before, being a cowboy and buying shampoo at the CVS Pharmacy? I was actually feeling kind of blue, forlorn, almost desperate. It was as if I thought I had to forget what had happened and just return to my humdrum life. Like there was no other alternative. Little did I know what was in store.

So I made some coffee and ate some cereal and cleaned up a little, vacuumed and put some stuff away, straightened up my bedroom and scrubbed the toilet. When I finished with my chores, I looked in the mirror and that's when it came to me. I could just keep on doing what I was doing. I was free. Nothing was stopping me except myself. This wasn't a one-shot deal: I could make it into a daily routine. Being that it made me feel so good and I wasn't hurting anyone, this seemed like a reasonable and even an obvious thing to do. So obvious it hadn't even occurred to me. Hidden in plain sight, once it had occurred to me, it immediately made me happy. I even started whistling and not only smiled, but laughed as well.

So I put the cowboy outfit back on and glued on the mustache and decided I would take the bus up to Hollywood Boulevard and drift among the tourists in front of Grauman's Chinese Theater. This would give me some variation on what I had already done and also heighten the risk of what I was doing. I wouldn't just be walking down to the local mall, I'd be right on Hollywood Boulevard with the drifters and the runaways and the guys who dress up as Spiderman and Superman and all the rest of the weirdos. And that would make for a good challenge for this here cowpoke.

On the way up Western Avenue, no one bothered me. One young man even offered me a seat but I declined: no cowboy needs a seat on the bus, no matter how old he is: he can stand up as well as anyone else, thank you very much. I got off on Hollywood Boulevard, changed buses and then disembarked at Highland. It was a bright blue day, a Tuesday, I believe, with that southern California sky shining up there like a polished plate. Everyone was walking around in shorts and a lot of them had their cameras out and they looked wide-eyed and bushy-tailed, seeing the sights of Hollywood. I caught some foreign languages, what sounded like Japanese or maybe it was Chinese or Korean, and then Russian as well, and I think some German too. People were gawking at everything, pointing out the names on the stars: Art Linkletter and Rin Tin Tin and Alan Ladd and Zsa Zsa Gabor. I'd always hated these stars, they were always getting grimy and sticky with dirt and mud. But, besides that, they just seemed so empty, as if names on a dirty sidewalk could conjure up anything resembling a real life. But maybe the real reason was envy and jealousy. Why weren't there stars for the nonentities and the anonymous? Hell, what about all the forgotten souls who labored at the DMV? Maybe they should have stars for them. Or what about janitors or busboys? Shouldn't others receive recognition besides these famous folks who had already spent their whole lives in the limelight?

Well, that was life. Never fair and no use whining about it. Though the idea of a walk of fame for the lonely and the neglected seemed right to me. Maybe I would contact someone in the city about it, call my council person, whoever that was, or maybe even write the mayor.

As I strolled up Hollywood Boulevard toward the Chinese

Theater, doing my best to maintain a Western kind of gait, the same stride I'd seen so many times in the movies and on television, a strange thing happened to me. Someone asked me if they could take a picture with me. At first I was startled and didn't know what to say. Then I smiled and said sure, that would be great. It was two ladies, one short with kind of tiny blue eyes, and the other medium height with brown eyes opening wide, and a pimply boy maybe about twelve, all of them kind of fat, especially the kid, and wearing t-shirts which they had probably just purchased because they were all themed around Los Angeles, the short lady with the Hollywood sign on her shirt, the brown-eyed one with a surfer girl, and then the kid with Disneyland on his. As we lined up for the photo, I asked them where they were from. "Wisconsin," one woman said, "Packer nation," said the other and then the kid, he added, "Cheese-head Land." "All right, cheese, I like it," I replied as I smiled for the I-phone.

Then another weird thing happened: one of the women asked me, "What movies have you been in?" I was completely startled again and didn't know what to say. But then I decided to just roll with it, as I didn't want to let them down. But there was something else to it too. I liked the idea of being an actor. Why shouldn't I be an actor? I was wearing a costume, after all. Judging from the results, tourists stopping me for pictures, then asking me what movies I've been in, it was working out pretty well, so what the heck: maybe I had been in pictures and wasn't even aware of it. Besides, a little fibbing never hurt anyone. "Well," I said, "my first picture was *High Plains Drifter* with Mister Clint Eastwood."

"Wow, you know him?" said the kid.

"Oh goodness, no," I replied. The kid looked kind of disappointed so I tried to backtrack on that one. "I mean, sure, we met. When we were making the movie. But I only had a couple of lines and, you know, he's a very busy man and all." I smiled.

Actually, I almost felt like I had met Eastwood and that I did have a few lines in *High Plains Drifter*. "Really a nice guy though. And what a professional. Always knew his lines." They looked up at me as if they expected more. And so I gave it to them: "And then I was in a movie called *Jaws*. I'm sure you know that one."

The short lady squealed with delight. "I love *Jaws*!" she screamed. Then she put down her head and opened her mouth wide, as if imitating the head of a shark. Her friend chimed in with her rendition of the theme from *Jaws*: "Doo dee doo dee doo!" she sang, laughing and squealing also. "I just about peed all over myself the first time I saw that one!" said the short lady, and the kid rolled his eyes and said, "Mom!" and his mother said, "Well, it's true, Hank," and then the other one said, "What part did you play in that one?" and the short one added, "I don't remember you," and I replied, with a forlorn tinge to my voice, "Cut out of the movie. Ended up on the editing floor," and they looked at me as if they were kind of bewildered, like they had no idea what it meant to be cut from a movie and to wind up on the editing floor. "They didn't use me in the final movie. The editor cut me out."

The short fat woman nodded slowly, as if the concept of being edited out of a movie was beginning to dawn on her.

"And then what happened?" the kid wanted to know.

I knew I had to work myself out of this, quick. "Well, I went to Europe and mostly worked in spaghetti westerns after that." Again, a look of total ignorance fell across the faces of the trio of Wisconsin tourists. So I tried to help them: "Westerns made in Italy. *Spaghetti* westerns."

"Oh, I see," said the kid. "So what's your name, anyway?"

I wasn't expecting that question and before I knew what I was saying, out popped: "Josh." I needed a last name too so I blurted out: "Hawley. Josh Hawley."

"Josh Hawley..." A dim sense of recognition began to form itself on the tall lady's face. "Gee, that sounds familiar..."

I began to move away, tipping my hat to indicate a Western-styled fare-thee-well. "Maybe you saw it in one of my films," I offered, turning around fast and moving into the crowd. "So long."

I walked quickly down Hollywood Boulevard, glancing over my shoulder now and then to make sure the folks from Wisconsin weren't trailing me or that the cops weren't following me, the tourists having complained to the police about a cowboy full of fibs. I was suddenly reminded of Robert de Niro as Travis Bickle in *Taxi Driver* when he runs away from the Secret Service men at that rally for the presidential candidate, Charles Whatever-His-Name-Was. A sheen of sweat had formed on my forehead: I took off my hat for a second to wipe it off and continued east towards Highland. Obviously, I needed to be much more prepared when I ventured forth into the unpredictability of the day. Blurting out the first name that came to my mind would not do. Josh Hawley! Christ! I was ashamed of myself and vowed to do better the next time I went forth into the crowd.

3

I decided to let the cowboy have one more chance. But I wanted to really work on his biography before I took him out again. Obviously, this was a necessity: I couldn't afford any more stupid mistakes. So I spent two entire days mapping out his life, giving him a name, giving him a mom and a dad and two brothers as well, one older and one younger, making up names and biographies for all of them, giving him a horse and a mule, and thinking about his guns and the gunfights he had had. I chose Provo, Utah, as his birthplace and Bisbee, Arizona, as the place where he'd spent the majority of his life. I decided he had drifted out to California to try his luck as a stunt rider and wrangler. I gave him a name too: Charlie McCoy. With a name like that, no one would question his authenticity.

The next morning I got up early and put on my costume. After I was done I looked in the bathroom mirror and really liked what I saw. Charlie McCoy was alive all right! I tried to suck in my gut so this old cowpoke wouldn't look like some fat jerk who lived on Whoppers, bacon cheeseburgers and fries. Not that I am fat. On the contrary, I've always been pretty slender, but I figured someone who had spent his entire life on the buttes and the plateaus and in the gullies and arroyos like Charlie McCoy has would be in great shape, even if his teeth had gone black from chewing on plugs of tobacco and his legs were bowed from so much time in the saddle. Finally, I put my Stetson on and smiled at myself in the mirror. I was ready.

I walked to the bus stop and waited for the 534. You might be wondering why a person living in L.A. isn't driving a car, this being such a car-crazy place. Thing is, I had given up driving when I turned sixty, just out of exhaustion with the traffic here. I couldn't take it anymore, the road rage and the maniacs driving like psychopaths behind the wheels of their various and sundry vehicles. Taking the bus gave me time to just stare out the window at the passing scenery or just people-watch at all the weird people who ride the MTA. I'll have to say, my stress-level has really lowered since I gave up the automobile.

Now I don't know if you've ever taken the bus to Malibu but it's an eye-opener. There were no other white people on the bus besides me. All Latinos except the bus driver, a black woman. It was pretty early in the morning, maybe seven-thirty or so, and there were maybe ten men on the bus and maybe twenty women. The women all looked like they were going to jobs as cleaning ladies and the guys looked like they were headed for manual labor jobs. Everyone was talking in Spanish so I didn't understand a thing they said, but they seemed pretty happy even if the looks on some of their faces were ones of fatigue.

Me, I was feeling great. I was headed for Malibu in my cowboy outfit. It was a glorious blue day and I was on an adventure. Pretty soon the Pacific Ocean came into view and I watched the waves come in and crash as the bus roared ahead. I made a game out of it: could I actually watch the full progress of a wave from its formation to its conclusion before the bus took me out of its sight? It actually only happened twice and each time it did I felt a certain triumph leap up in my throat. In fact, the second time it happened, I let out a "Yes!" and pumped my fist. One of the Mexican ladies turned around and looked at me curiously when I did this. I'm sure I blushed and then I muttered something like, "It's just…" or maybe I just said "Hi," I can't remember. Then she turned back around and I looked out the window and made a vow not to lose control of myself again.

When we got to Malibu Village, the first thing I did was go into Starbucks. I needed some coffee, but more than that I was hoping I might see a celebrity there. I had once seen Dick Van Dyke at a Starbucks in Culver City and maybe something along those lines would happen here. It wasn't just that I simply wanted to see a celebrity, though that was certainly part of what I wanted to do. I mean who doesn't like spotting someone famous, even if you do live in L.A. and you've gotten pretty used to seeing celebrities every once in a while and you are kind of sick and tired of the celebrities being the only folks who get to be famous. But the main reason I was hoping I'd see someone famous, especially an actor or an actress, was that I figured they were experts and specialists in costumes and disguises and that if I could get away with it in front of them, then I could get away with my cowboy outfit in front of anyone. Unfortunately, even though I lingered in Starbucks for almost an hour, getting a refill and nursing it slowly along, no one important entered the coffee shop. Well, at least no one important that I recognized. Yet it was a success, nevertheless, because certainly the customers and the staff that did see me didn't raise any alarms or even seem to look twice. I was a cowboy. I was Charlie McCoy. I wasn't Lloyd Stollman, ex-DMV employee, fresh out of twenty-five years in an anonymous cubicle. I was a cowboy, fresh off the range.

When I left Starbucks, I crossed the PCH and headed down to the beach. There weren't too many people down there. It was a weekday, after all, and the weather was not the greatest, as it had suddenly gone a little overcast and gloomy. There were a couple of surfers out there and a few people on their own walking up and down the beach. I stood there, watching the gulls arc and swerve across the sky. Then I decided to stroll down the beach a little and see what I could see. My boots were a bit uncomfortable there on the sand, but I didn't want to take them off as what would I do with them then? I didn't want to carry them along with me, as that would look silly and be too much of a load and I couldn't just hide them somewhere on the beach as they might be stolen and then where would I be, what with no shoes on my feet, a cowboy heading home on the bus bare-footed?

As I walked down the beach and then rounded a point and continued south, I noticed a very lean, well-built man with blonde hair jogging my way. Something about him seemed very familiar, as if we'd been friends long ago or as if he was a figure from out of a dream. But as we got closer to each other I realized I had seen him in the movies and that it was Matthew McConaughey. I couldn't believe my luck! This would really be a great test as here was a renowned actor who had worn all sorts of costumes and disguises and, besides, if my memory served me right, he was from Texas and so would know all about genuine cowboys. If I could pass as a real cowboy in front of Matthew McConaughey, then I could pass as a cowboy in front of anyone. I screwed up all the courage I could muster and as McConaughey approached me I raised my hand and waved, "Hello, Mister McConaughey," I said, "I'm a big fan."

"Thanks," he said, flashing that million-dollar smile as he ran past.

Before I could stop myself, I turned and added, pretty much shouting it out: "My name's Charlie McCoy! I'm a real cowboy!"

I don't know why I said that or what I was expecting McConaughey to do but I blurted it out nonetheless. Of course McConaughey didn't respond: he just kept running up the beach. I turned away as quickly as possible, ashamed of my silly outburst. I had to be more careful. But I got so excited about the possibilities of my role that I made idiotic blunders. Still, I had to learn to be disciplined, like an actor who follows stage directions and recites his lines. They don't abruptly decide to shift gears and crash reality right into fantasy; they stick with the dimensions staked out by the writer and the director for their character as it's laid out in the script. Imagine if McConaughey had turned around and engaged in a conversation with me about horses or cattle, Appaloosas and mustangs, heifers and bulls. Suppose he had asked me where my own horse was, and why I was in Malibu, strolling down the beach in my cowboy boots, and had I ever been in Nevada or New Mexico or Arizona or Texas and what did I think about the Bureau of Land Management and their policy with wild horses.

Suddenly I stopped and turned and looked out over the blue sheen of the ocean. Matthew McConaughey, the movie star, I had just seen him. Not only had I just seen him, but I had introduced myself to him and we had exchanged words. I had just seen a celebrity, a real one, fame his constant companion, his face known to millions, his voice coming out of that silver screen all over the world and his image entering the eyes of all those people in the dark staring up at the screen. He was a movie star. He was a real, honest-to-god movie star and I had just seen him running on the beach. And I had told him my name and that I was a real cowboy. And McConaughey hadn't done anything, I mean he hadn't contradicted what I had said. He hadn't turned on me and said, in a vaguely or maybe even downright threatening voice, "You're no cowboy. You're a fake and I bet your name isn't even Charlie McCoy, it's probably something like Bruce Smith or Robert Mullins or Earl Fuller." No, none of that had happened. He had just continued on jogging down the beach, which could be interpreted as an implicit or even an explicit agreement with all that he had heard.

Abruptly I had the impulse to turn and start running back up the beach to catch up with McConaughey so I could find out for sure if he had believed me. But no, that would be ridiculous, I would just be harassing him like some crazy fan with a pen looking for an autograph. Besides, I was in my cowboy boots and how fast could I run up a beach anyway? No, I'd never catch the movie star. I had lost my chance. All of a sudden, I felt terrifically depressed. Fame had been there right beside me and I had let it slip by. Somehow I should have extended the conversation. After all, McConaughey's "Thanks" had sounded real and genuine, as if it was an open invite to more conversation, a real dialogue, maybe even a friendship. Or at least an acquaintanceship. But I had blown it. I could have been friends with a movie star but now I was just a nobody in a cowboy suit. Anonymous, alone, bereft, a zero, a nonentity who had spent twenty-five years working at the DMV and was now calling himself Charlie McCoy and was dressed up like a goddamn cowboy. What kind of fucking fool was I?

I got up off the beach as soon as I could, found myself a bus stop, and waited for the bus to come. A convertible full of teenagers in nothing but swim suits roared past and one of them yelled out, "Howdy, cowboy! Eat any bullshit lately?" The laughter of the teenagers sailed over the sound of the engine as the car disappeared down the PCH. Fucking kids. No respect. Not even for a cowboy in a Stetson hat. I would show them. Yes, I would.

4

Wanting to broaden my horizons, I sat in front of my bathroom mirror and made faces. After all, I didn't want to be a cowboy for the rest of my life. If I squished my eyes together, I could be Chinese. If I put a real hard look in my eyes, I could be a thief or maybe even a murderer, especially if I didn't allow even a hint of a smile to cross my face. Or I could be a businessman, that is, if I put on my suit and tie and squared up in front of the mirror, looking very serious and enterprising and trustworthy indeed.

But I thought that what I really needed if I was going to pull this off was some makeup and maybe even a wig or two. I Googled "Hollywood makeup" and found a place up on Hollywood Boulevard which carried both makeup of a wide variety and a good selection of wigs.

The next day I took the bus up to Hollywood and perused the aisles of the store I had located on Google. A very nice young lady with a pierced nose and blue makeup on one cheek and black on the other asked me if I needed any help and I said yes, I most certainly did. She got me equipped with a basic makeup kit—eyeliner, shadow, pancake, cold cream—and then she showed me the wigs. What I wasn't expecting, and it's kind of stupid on my part that I didn't expect this, was that female wigs outnumbered male wigs about fifty to one. The thought of dressing up like a female had never occurred to me before but suddenly with a long row of mannequin heads donned in blonde and brunette wigs, Afros and even a bouffant, the idea of costuming myself as a female seemed attractive. Not just attractive—that's too weak a word—

but challenging, so much so that it seemed thrilling. If I could successfully pass myself off as, say, a blonde woman of forty, then I could do anything. Still, I didn't want to overplay my hand. So along with the makeup, I bought a black toupee and a blonde wig. At the register, the cashier asked if I was an actor. "Of sorts," I replied, smiling. She smiled back and said, "I know just what you mean."

Outside, in the bright sunlight, I put my sunglasses on and walked down the sidewalk towards the bus stop on Vine. I held the bag tightly in my hand. People passing didn't know I had two wigs and a makeup kit in there. That was my little secret. It made me feel alive.

5

The next morning I had a hard time deciding what to do. Should I just go out with my own face on as a disguise or should I use my new purchases to disguise myself? Over cereal and coffee I debated the pros and cons in my head but then finally let my gut make the choice.

The black toupee looked good on me in the bathroom mirror. It was snug on my head and shaved maybe fifteen or twenty years off of me, turning me into a middle-aged man instead of the senior citizen I was getting to be. But besides that, in my estimation at least, it made me look handsome. Well, maybe not handsome, but pretty good-looking. It gave me a kind of jaunty look, that jet black toupee. I could actually see myself maybe meeting a woman and dating her, wearing this thing, but then a moment later that vanished from my mind as I realized I would still have the same inhibitions, no matter what was on top of my head. But maybe that was wrong too. Maybe the toupee would liberate me, at least to a certain degree, at least to the extent that I might be able to talk to a woman and maybe even ask her out for dinner.

I thought I'd wear a nice collared shirt with the toupee and maybe creased slacks and my best shoes, black wingtips polished to a high sheen. When I got everything on, I felt awfully good, as if the clothes matched the toupee, the toupee matched the clothes, and everything matched me. I took one last look in the mirror, patted the toupee down, smiled, and then headed out for my adventure. I figured this guy as a hustler, maybe the card shark type, definitely someone you might see in Vegas, working the tables, playing craps or blackjack. He was what you might call a smooth operator, sharp, well-groomed, a lady's man, something I had never been and something I had always wanted to be. I made a mental note to myself not to let this last item get out of hand—I didn't want this character making any advances on women, not with my lack of knowledge about such things. But maybe after I had taken him out on the streets a few times, maybe then I could try him out on a female. 'Cause it just could be that he could give me the courage and the words I had always lacked.

I decided this guy belonged in Beverly Hills, so I took the Western 207 up to Wilshire and then transferred to the Wilshire Express. The bus ride was uneventful except that a man carrying two shopping bags kept muttering to himself about the gutters of Hell, black sluiceways, he called them, in which sinners would be deposited once their lives had ended, as the Lord and the Devil were distributors of absolute justice which no man or woman could escape, so everyone better straighten out or the black throughways of Hell would chuckle when they embraced the bodies and the souls of the damned. I moved away from this maniac and sat in the back where the madman's mumbling was just a string of unintelligible consonants and vowels.

Outside the window, the city swept by. Hard to believe that I had spent my whole adult life in this place. And without ever once feeling that it was home. Such an alien place, what with every building never lasting more than twenty years or so, giving the landscape a permanent temporary feel, as if everything could disappear tomorrow and no one would even know the difference. Oh, the smog had gotten better and the crime wasn't as bad as it had been in the 1980s and the 1990s but it was still a surreal and strange town. A place where friends were hard to make, at least for me. I had had one friend, though, a co-worker of mine at the DMV, Dorothy Ward. We used to do stuff together, go to the movies and once or twice even a Dodgers game. Once we even went so far as to plan a trip to Mammoth but she backed out, saying her parents were sick and she needed to tend to them. But I didn't believe her. There was something too nervous in her voice when she gave me this news, something too quivery and wavering in her delivery and her tone, like she was trying to hide something. That kind of soured the relationship, and then soon after she moved to Delaware. I always thought Dorothy's move had something to do with that busted-up trip to Mammoth but that's probably wrong, as it puts too much emphasis on something that I don't think meant that much to begin with.

Okay, I'll confess: I also go to a Thai massage parlor once a month and get a rubdown finished off with what I guess you'd call a hand job. It's kind of seedy, I know, and somewhat embarrassing too, but I have to do something to relieve myself. There is one girl there who I got stuck on. Her name is Ting. A really nice girl from Bangkok. Can hardly speak a word of English, but she has the sweetest smile and is always very gentle with me. I guess you could say I'm one of her regulars.

So that is it for me and relationships. Loneliness has been my lot. And I don't mean for that to sound like I'm full of self-pity, though it probably does sound that way, regardless. Being alone has its benefits. No one trying to tell you what to do. No complications about plans. You just make them and follow them, or not, and there's no repercussions or ramifications, at least in a personal way. And no one disappointed with you if you don't live up to their expectations. Plus, it's much quieter. No one trying to impose their ideas of right and wrong on you. Why, imagine if I lived with someone, what would they say if I walked out of the house in my cowboy costume or with a toupee stuck on my head?

When I got off the bus at Beverly and Wilshire, I decided

to stroll up into the commercial district of Beverly Hills just to see what I could see and try and notice if anyone looked at me funny, what with the toupee and everything. But though I passed plenty of people, some of them Asian tourists gawking at all the expensive stores, some of them looking like Beverly Hills housewives on their way to appointments, maybe to dermatologists for Botox injections, and some of them young white men with sharp haircuts and eager faces, maybe young show business types trying to make it in this town, no one took a second look at me.

I had done it again. My disguise had worked. I was free. I could be anyone I wanted to be. Sure, I'd have to spend more money and maybe do some research on the Internet about applying makeup and stuff, but all that was no problem. I have a good pension and Social Security, plus my wants and needs are very minimal, and making money a minor issue. Researching on the web was no problem either, as working at the DMV for twenty-five years had made me pretty Internet-savvy. So the possibilities loomed large. In fact, they were dizzying. I could be anybody! That was one side of the equation. I didn't have to be me anymore! That was the other side of the equation.

Realizing the magnitude of all this, I almost fainted right there on Rodeo Drive. In fact, I did stumble a little and I had to lean against a lamppost to remain upright. Standing there, trying to get my breath back, the whirlpool of possibilities spun through my head. Maybe I could even be a black person, or at least someone brown. Being a woman seemed like a definite possibility, though I knew that would require a lot of preparation before I could take her out on the street. I could be a riverboat gambler maybe or a plumber or a cook or maybe even a clown, though of course that would attract too much attention, so I quickly discarded that notion. Damn, I was getting too excited with all the alternatives suddenly available to me and I wasn't thinking straight. I just had to be what I was right now, a middle-aged slick card shark who spent most of his time shooting craps and the rest of his time at the track or chasing the girls. He was a cool character who didn't take shit from anyone. And he knew that everyone was playing a game, life was just one big con with winners and losers, and the winners were those who stayed focused and cool and who most of all were in on the joke that everyone was running a con. Then all that was needed was a perspective on the odds of everyone's game and the courage to place your bets down accordingly.

I got coffee at a little place on Rexford. The waitress didn't seem to look at me funny. She just accepted me exactly as I was. She was cute too. A brunette with a nice little figure and long legs that looked absolutely delicious. What was odd was that I was reacting to this woman through the lens of my disguise. I didn't look at girls this way, with a kind of lustful perspective. But evidentially the character I was playing did: he noticed those long legs whereas I had long ago stopped gawking at women. But that all made sense, as I was inside another person now, I was living in my disguise and so of course I thought that way. As a matter of fact, seeing the waitress the way I was seeing her, through the eyes of my Las Vegas disguise, just verified the direction I was already on as if I had really stepped into another life and was doing a pretty damn good job of it too.

When the waitress came by for a refill, before I even thought about it, I blurted out, "You must get great tips." She looked at me and smiled. "Why do you say that?" she asked. "I got vision," I said. "I can see." She blushed and I think I may have blushed as well. I couldn't believe I had said this. But then it was wasn't really me saying it, was it? "Well, I don't know whether to slap you or say thanks," she said, still smiling. "Why don't you say yes," I suggested. "Yes to what?" she asked. "Yes to going out with me on Saturday night." Again, this had just popped out and I realized as well that I was speaking in some sort of accent, maybe halfway between a New York City and a Chicago accent, something very urban and kind of smacking of the criminal. But my own accent was mixed in there as well, so it sounded kind of like a lousy actor trying to imitate Robert de Niro or something. I made a mental note to do some work on this and then my little pause of self-criticism was interrupted by the waitress: "You work pretty fast, don't you?"

I smiled at her. I was back in character and that was good. "Life's too short. You gotta go fast."

"Well, there's fast," she said, "and then there's fast. Your speed is way too quick for me."

I kept my smile fastened on her. I was undressing her with my eyes and she looked good. "Don't worry, sister. I can go slow too." My voice seemed to have taken on a soft, seductive quality, the quality of a wolf, a womanizer, a cad. But slick and cool, not too overt with the flirtatious overtones, playing it just right. "And then maybe we can get our speeds adjusted so they fit right into a nice little tight groove together." I wasn't sure where that line had come from, but there it was, spoken with that same soft, smooth quality.

She laughed loudly, one big hoot. "Wow, you are too much, mister." She turned away and walked to the kitchen, shaking her head. Maybe I had gone a little too far, but on the other hand, I had laid my cards on the table. I certainly hadn't wimped out, which was my usual style. This Vegas guy didn't fool around. He knew what he wanted and he went for it. And if someone else didn't like what was happening, so what. That was their problem, not Buddy's.

Buddy? Who the hell was that?

Yes, of course, this guy needed a name. Buddy was right. In

fact, Buddy was perfect. Last name? Dicks. No, sounded like a porn star: Buddy Dicks. Buddy Dickenson. Nope, too dang long. Then I heard it: Buddy Dickson. That had the right ring. I could see Buddy Dickson saying something like, My name is Buddy Dickson, and no one saying a word. Buddy Dickson, card shark. Buddy Dickson, chaser of female tail. Buddy Dickson, pal of the wise guys in the Mob. Buddy Dickson, legendary in Vegas and well known in Chicago, Kansas City and New York. Buddy Dickson. With a name like that, the world better watch out.

I dropped a five on the table, leaving a three dollar tip, and headed for the exit. As I walked down the street, I felt big and confident and bold. Again this expansive feeling came over me, the feeling that I could do anything, be anybody. As long as I maintained a solid belief in what I was doing, everything would be fine. The really amazing part was that I had not discovered this about myself until I had retired. All those years of slumber at the DMV now seemed like a dream, an elongated period of unconsciousness until I woke up when I became Charlie McCoy and then Buddy Dickson.

And me and Buddy Dickson were doing just fine, thank you. Striding across the streets of Beverly Hills, winking at the girls and giving the men a look of cold steel as if I'd kill them just as soon as say hello. When Buddy Dickson walked down a street, he was in charge of that street. He didn't make way for anyone, he didn't cringe or freeze in fear. It was up to other people to be afraid because Buddy Dickson was in town. The people on the sidewalk seemed to get this message as the men looked away as if trying to avoid the look in my eyes, and the women tried to hide their smiles like they couldn't help but like a man like Buddy Dickson, a real man, a man who took no crap from nobody, a connected man, a man who would have been right at home in a movie like *The Godfather* or *Wise Guys* or *Bugsy*.

I decided to stop at one of the fancy clothing stores on Rodeo Drive and maybe get Buddy a shirt or cuff links or something. So I ducked into this place, just wanting to browse really, but before I even had a chance, this young mutt was on me, asking me how I was, telling me his name was Ted and was everything fine and that if I needed any assistance just to let him, that is, Ted, know and he would be available instantaneously and being as obsequious as obsequious can be, and me, I attributed all this to the aura of Buddy Dickson, the way he carried himself, his jet black hair and his sharp clothes and the self-assured look in his eye. I just moseyed slow around the store, glancing dismissively at three-hundred-dollar shirts, turning up my nose at hand-tailored Italian slacks, and not even looking at the display case full of gold and silver cuff links, so that when I walked out of there the general impression left behind was one of stunned disbelief: who was that guy? Did you see him? The way he walked. His clothes. His hair. That guy was straight Mafia, a made man, no doubt about it.

Riding the bus home, everything was fine. At least for a while. I was just sitting in the back of the bus, minding my own business, staring out the window and reflecting on all the possibilities my new life was bestowing upon me when I heard a racket up toward the front of the bus. A male voice cried out, "Bitch! You know who you're fucking with?!" and then a female voice shouted out in response: "Yes, I know who I'm fucking with—a raggedy-ass fucking nigger who needs to get his sorry butt off the street." Then I could see a young black man pushing an older black lady and I stood up and moved up the aisle as this was something that someone like Buddy Dickson would never abide, not in a million years. And since I was not only like Buddy Dickson, but I was Buddy Dickson, I was going to have to do something about it, pronto. So before I even had time to consider what I was doing, the risks I was taking and the danger I was putting myself in, I was right in the face of this young black man who seemed to be high on something and whose teeth were discolored and his hair full of dirt and fuzz and completely askew. "What the fuck you want, white man?" he growled.

"I want you to quit whatever the fuck it is you are doing, motherfucker," I replied. The black man had swung his body out into the aisle and now he was facing me in a kind of parody of a fighter's stance, his arms waving in front of his face, his hands bundled into fists, his feet shifting one to the other. The victim of his attack was sitting in the adjacent seat, her face turned to the window. The black man took a wild swing at me and I easily ducked out of the way. "Okay, that's it," called out the bus driver, "I'm pulling over and I'm calling the cops." The bus swerved to the curb as all the passengers stared at this showdown in the middle of the aisle. The black man pushed his way to the door and shoved on it once, twice and then on the third time it opened and he made a move to leap off the bus. But at the last moment, he leaned back into the bus, reached out his arm and ripped the toupee off my head. "Yes," he cried out triumphantly, "just what I thought. White man's wearing himself a rug." He threw the toupee down on the floor of the bus and then jumped off the bus, laughing wildly as he did so. I grabbed the toupee and pivoted around, staring at everyone on the bus. Some of the passengers had looks of horror on their face, as if a weird roadside oddity had just been revealed to them, a two-headed ox or a seven-fingered dwarf or something like that. Others were looking away, as if they were so embarrassed, they couldn't stand the sight of this suddenly de-wigged old white man. Still others were pointing at me and beginning to laugh as if this was the funniest thing they had ever seen, the toupee ripped off the head of this man who had been trying to be such a big hero. The laughers won, as those who were horrified and those who were embarrassed all started, at first slowly and softly, but soon rapidly and loudly, to laugh at this sad white man stripped bare of his wig who was standing there frozen in the middle of the aisle. Even the driver was laughing at me, his laughter actually the loudest of all. This horrible moment probably lasted no longer than five seconds but it seemed like hours or days or even weeks to me, the whole thing moving past in elongated slow-motion horror.

I tore myself away from my frozen spot there on the bus and raced out the open door. I hit the ground running, my wig in my hand. I could see the young black man up ahead—we were in the middle of Koreatown at about 5th Street and Western Avenue. He was headed down Western towards Wilshire and I followed after. He ducked into the Metro station, taking three steps at a time down the escalator. He jumped over the turn style, laughing, and I pushed my Tap card on the style, swiveled through, and made my way down the stairs as quickly as I could. But the young black man must have already gotten inside the train because I didn't see him anymore and the train was pulling away from the station. I stood there in the middle of the platform, the toupee in my hand, swiveling left and right, looking every which way. As the last car passed by, I caught a glimpse of the black guy in the train window. He made a small little wave at me, sort of like Frog One in *The French Connection*. But he wasn't smiling like Frog One. He was laughing. The train moved into the tunnel and I turned away and made my way up the stairs. It was a long walk home.

6

Obviously, something had to change. I wasn't going to be caught like that again. Humiliated, my disguise exposed, everyone on the bus laughing at me, even the bus driver. I thought about giving up the whole thing. It was just too risky. I couldn't afford that level of exposure, or even the possibility of that level of shame. Still, when it worked (and it had worked most of the time), it was incredible, liberating, sublime. Maybe that one incident had been an exception. And maybe if I just planned things out a little better I could protect myself against such consequences. I had to give it another try. The rewards were so overwhelming, the thrill of it all, the feeling of being lost in someone else, the craziness and wonder when other people took my disguise as real—it was too much to surrender. Still, I had to prepare for anything and I had to protect myself as well. These things were obvious and so I started to work on them.

I spent the next two weeks in intense study and preparation. I took out books from the library on acting, I surfed through the Internet and found several manuals on makeup and wigs, and I got into character and practiced in my house, utterly losing myself in my roles, prepping myself for any and all eventualities, standing in front of the mirror and trying my makeup on, fitting my wigs just so, trying out accents and dialects, and so on. Then I took out my best kitchen knife and sharpened it, honing the edge until it practically gleamed. I made a kind of sheath for the knife, a leather holster which fit nicely underneath my coat. I practiced moves with the knife, whipping it out of its case and arcing it around until I was ready for anything that might come my way. Here I was reminded of *Taxi Driver* again, and Travis Bickle in his seedy little apartment, sharpening his knife and practicing his moves. But of course this was a lot different. Travis Bickle is a fictional character. I am real.

After two weeks I was ready to go out on the street again. I had developed a character I called Frank Bunyan, a swarthy retired trucker who didn't take shit from nobody and talked in a kind of low growl. Frank Bunyan wore blue jeans or black work pants, Dickies, and plaid shirts and black motorcycle boots and sometimes he wore a blue wool cap pulled down low on his head. Frank Bunyan was always ready for anything and he'd been in every state in the continental United States, driving semis coast to coast, picking up whores in truck stops, playing craps in the back rooms of diners, and pulling off a few jobs along the way, boosting loads from off the backs of trailers and selling them to fences in New Orleans and Memphis. Frank Bunyan was a guy who knew his way around and wasn't going to be pushed around by nobody, regardless if they were twenty and he was sixty-two, it didn't matter, Frank Bunyan could still handle himself, no doubt about that. And no doubt about it, Frank Bunyan could handle a gun or a knife: he'd done so before and he could do it again.

I decided to let Frank Bunyan loose in the Crenshaw district so I took the bus down Washington to Crenshaw and then transferred onto the 207. I got off at Stocker or maybe I should say, Frank Bunyan and I got off there, as Frank and I had fused together, the one commingled so far with the other that the difference was hard, if not impossible, to gauge.

I walked through the streets of the Crenshaw, Frank Bunyan leading the way. I didn't know what I was looking for. I think I just wanted to see if Bunyan could pass the test of reality, if he could move through the streets of a predominantly black neighborhood without detection, without undue notice, without anyone trying to unmask him. And I felt good, confident, cool. I noticed that my stride was longer than usual, that Frank Bunyan walked with the gait of a trucker, a little stooped over from all that time sitting in the cab of the truck as he drove that old semi coast to coast, yet his stride unbowed, full throttled, velocity steady as he moved across Crenshaw into Leimert Park.

The park itself is mostly full of homeless black guys, cardboard shacks and pup tents sheltering the poor and the unfortunate, crazy, muttering men, high on crack and cheap wine and whiskey. I walked through it and felt my mysterious presence creating a path that fell open in front of me. There was a charisma to Frank Bunyan, a feeling of power that I had certainly never felt as Lloyd Stollman, twenty-five years at the DMV, dutifully snapping photos of all those people, even now their faces sweeping through my mind, an endless collage of them, big ones and bony ones, sad ones and happy ones, the young and the old, the black and the white, and one lady who cried as her picture was taken, maybe because her best days were behind her and having her photo snapped was only a reminder of her former glory. I remember telling her softly not to worry, there is a beauty in aging, but perhaps I never said that at all and only think that I did.

I found an empty bench, sat down and surveyed the scene. Of course Frank Bunyan could see the details of the situation much better than I could. He was a trucker. He had lived on the road all his life. He had seen all sorts of things that I couldn't even imagine. I was only a clerk at the DMV, whereas Frank Bunyan was a big-rig driver who had witnessed shit going down in every state in the contiguous United States. So, naturally, I deferred to his judgment. So that when one of the homeless guys in the park asked for a handout, I followed Frank's lead and handed the guy a buck. Me, I would never have even been there in the first place, let alone given this scraggly guy a whole dollar. "Thanks, friend," the homeless man muttered, smiling. "It's nothing," I replied, and really, it was nothing. I had plenty of money. Not that I was rich but I had a pension and some savings. I mean I could certainly afford to give this poor guy a buck, that's for sure. And Frank Bunyan, he was generous. He had a big heart. He had had some hard times himself, like when his first wife. Eileen, died in a car accident and when his second wife, Janis, passed on due to cancer. These things had crushed him at the time, almost to the point where he felt like killing himself, it got so gloomy. But he had weathered the storm and now here he was, man enough to walk right into the heart of the Crenshaw "jungle," and humanitarian enough to give a guy a handout when it was needed. Not that Frank Bunyan would think of himself as a humanitarian. He didn't need such a fancy title. He was just a man, like others, that was all.

Yet, sitting there in Leimert Park, watching the homeless men while away their time as they endured another day, there was something else to Frank Bunyan as well. He fit into his skin. He was Frank Bunyan and that's all he was. He didn't need to complain about anything. He didn't need to wallow in self-pity or fester in anger. He was fine just as he was. A retired trucker with maybe five million miles behind him and maybe many more miles ahead, depending on luck and circumstance.

I stood up and stretched and Frank Bunyan was right there with me, yawning and walking through the park. Frank Bunyan was my companion. He was my friend. We could walk around together. My whole life I had been lonely and now I had a host of friends, Charlie McCoy and Buddy Dickson and Frank Bunyan. And that wasn't the end of it. I could have as many friends as I wanted. It was all up to my imagination and my skill as an impersonator. But no, that's not right, I wasn't an impersonator, there was no real Charlie McCoy or Buddy Dickson or Frank Bunyan to impersonate. These were creations, brought forth from my mind. Yet they were real. Actually, more real than real people, at least to me. Maybe it was an art form, a new one I was creating all on my own.

I felt good on the bus ride home. I would never be alone again. I could have as many friends as I wanted. The prospect was so exciting. I hadn't been this happy since I was a kid.

7

So it had worked. No complications, no interference, no obstacles, no nothing. Taking Frank Bunyan out on the street had revived my self-confidence, giving me the assurance that I was on the right path and that my life's work was creating these characters, these alter egos, these fragments of myself and inserting them into society at street level, right on the ground, as it were. And, once again, I was thrilled when contemplating the range of parts I could play, the depths and the heights I could reach. This was the real way to explore the human psyche. Acting really didn't go far enough, as actors and actresses confined their work to a stage or a studio. I was going out into real actuality with my characters; I was using life as my stage, Los Angeles and its environs were my studio. It seemed to me that what I was doing required much more bravery and skill than what's needed by an actor. Actors and actresses play it safe, surrounding themselves by all these elements that guard them against the rough edges of reality. They have directors and lighting people and makeup artists and personal assistants and all these buffers to cushion any blow that actually might come their way. Me, I was out in the open, raw, savage, the borders between fiction and fact completely ripped apart. What I was doing was basically a new art form, with me as its pioneer. And I truly believe that if it hadn't ended the way it did, there would be masses of people following in my footsteps. But that's another story…

The upshot of successfully taking Frank Bunyan out on the streets was that I felt I could risk bringing back Buddy Dickson and letting him loose again. I didn't want to accept the way Buddy's brief life had concluded, what with his toupee ripped off his head right in the middle of the bus. Buddy deserved better. And I was going to give it to him. Besides, Buddy had a hankering to visit that waitress back in Beverly Hills and I couldn't deny the hunger prowling through Buddy Dickson's loins.

So the next day I put Buddy Dickson on, this time making absolutely certain Buddy's toupee was so stuck to my head it couldn't be pried loose by anyone. As a matter of fact, I had got it so stuck to my skull, I wasn't one hundred percent certain I would be able to get it off. After I had checked, double-checked and even triple-checked myself in the mirror, and once I was sure I had Buddy's Chicago-New Jersey tough guy accent down, I went out my front door and began to make my way to the intersection of Western Avenue and Venice Boulevard where I would catch the 207 up to Wilshire.

I should say something about my neighbors and the precautions I took against their suddenly seeing strange characters coming out of my front door. First of all, I barely knew my neighbors, even though I had lived in the same place for eleven years. I'm just not a friendly neighborhood kind of a guy. I like my anonymity and I assume you like yours, so let's just leave one another alone, that's my credo. Still, I did have a nodding acquaintance with a few of my neighbors, even if that acquaintance was a begrudging one, at least on my part. So I always peeked out the curtain of the front door before I headed for the sidewalk, making sure the coast was clear. One time a neighbor did catch me coming out the front door dressed as Benny Monger and I had to make a critical snap judgment about what to do, but we'll get to that later, considering I haven't even brought Benny Monger onto the stage yet. Anyway, the day I am recounting to you now, the day I took Buddy Dickson back to Beverly Hills, I did make sure the coast was clear, and we strolled up Wilton Place together without anyone seeing anything.

The bus ride to Beverly Hills was uneventful and therefore successful. No one cast a dubious look my way. No one even glanced at me. The bus driver even smiled at me when I boarded. As we sailed down Wilshire I was beaming inside. I was Buddy Dickson again and Buddy Dickson was me. And what was Buddy Dickson doing? Why, he was headed back to that Beverly Hills diner to make some time with that waitress with the gorgeous gams.

Arrived at the diner, I sat down and waited for that pretty little thing to make her appearance. And she didn't let me down. As a matter of fact, as soon as she saw me, she broke into a smile that really warmed my heart and sent an unmistakable signal that I had made the right choice in bringing Buddy Dickson back to this joint. "So one time wasn't enough?" she said to me when she came up to my table, her pad in her left hand, pencil in her right, her hips kind of stuck out at a sexy angle, letting me know she was ready for whatever I could bring her way.

"No, you're right," I answered. "One time was not enough."

For a moment we just stayed right there, a suspended kind of a moment, smiling at each other, the sexual energy tingling all over.

"What do you want?"

"Let me see," I said softly, looking her up and down. "What do I want?"

"What do you want…from the menu," she said, at once encouraging and discouraging me, as the flirtatious look in her eye belied the direction of her words.

"And what if all I want is you?" I couldn't quite believe I had said this but then of course it was Buddy Dickson and not me speaking.

The waitress actually blushed, a sheet of crimson sweeping fast across her face. "You might have to wait for that, my friend," she replied.

"Oh? What time do you get off?" I answered. Buddy Dickson was amazing. Man, he worked quickly.

"When the last sip of coffee has been swallowed and the last piece of toast has been—"

"Six o'clock?" he asked. "That's what the sign on the door says." Buddy's devilish grin could not be wiped off his face. That grin was like an open invitation for sex. If it was me, I would've just fled. Hell, I never would've come into the joint in the first place, let alone had the balls to talk to this girl.

"Yeah," said the waitress and the grin on her face couldn't be wiped away, even if she had wanted it to: Buddy Dickson's roguish charm was simply overwhelming and wouldn't be denied. "Six o'clock."

"What's your name anyway, gorgeous?" asked Buddy.

"Rita. Rita White," said the Beverly Hills waitress, extending her hand.

Buddy took her hand, turned it over and kissed it. What style! What charm! Where did Buddy come up with these things. "And me," Buddy said, "I am Buddy Dickson."

"Buddy Dickson, huh?" the waitress said as if she wasn't quite certain that this was actually Buddy's name. A tremor of paranoia rushed through me. Perhaps I had been discovered. Perhaps she knew. But no…

"Buddy Dickson," she said again, and the twinge of suspicion had dropped out of her voice. "I like that. Got a ring."

"Don't it," replied Buddy. "But Rita White and Buddy Dickson: that ain't just a ring, that's a symphony."

Rita blushed again. `"Wow," she said, "you really are

something."

"Six o'clock?" said Buddy, dropping a ten-dollar bill on his table.

"Six o'clock," said Rita, smiling.

8

Buddy had two hours to kill and he didn't quite know what to do. I had heard that the bar at the Beverly Wilshire Hotel was a place where the bold and the beautiful liked to drink, and, as I certainly thought Buddy fit within that classification, we headed to the hotel and a scotch on the rocks at the bar. It's a dimly lit elegant place with a grand piano in one corner and someone was playing some of the great American standards while Buddy nursed his drink. The piano player was a middle-aged black woman, quite beautiful, her face shining as she played "Some Enchanted Evening" and "Autumn in New York" and "Smoke Gets in Your Eyes," and so on. It made for the perfect ambience, what with the ice tinkling in Buddy's glass and the dim light of the Beverly Hills afternoon filtering through the red curtains and the piano player with her gorgeous skin and the couple in the corner booth necking while the bartender smiled.

I couldn't quite believe I was here with Buddy. Well, actually, I couldn't quite believe I was in a bar at all. I never went to bars, let alone a fancy Beverly Hills bar like this. If I drank, I drank alone at home. But now that I was Buddy Dickson, I had been emancipated from such mundane constraints. This was Buddy Dickson's milieu. This was Buddy Dickson's natural habitat. Buddy Dickson was scotch on the rocks. Buddy Dickson was "Stardust" and "Baltimore Oriole" and "Just One of Those Things." Buddy Dickson was the Beverly Wilshire Hotel.

I ordered another drink and Buddy drank it. Buddy could drink but I couldn't, so the second drink was one drink too many for me and I was starting to get a little tipsy by the time to exit the bar rolled around. Buddy left a ten-dollar tip for the bartender and a twenty for the piano player who smiled up at him as she launched into "My Funny Valentine." When Buddy and I stepped outside, the bright light temporarily blinded us and we weren't sure which way the diner was. But then we got our bearings and strolled over to the place, whistling and humming some of the tunes we had heard in the bar.

Rita White was just coming out of the diner when Buddy Dickson and I walked up. Buddy had perfect timing, that much was obvious. "Well, you're right on time," said Rita, smiling.

"Not going to keep my baby waiting," Buddy said with this nonchalant ease. Rita blushed a little and then asked, '"My baby"'?

"Sure," said Buddy, taking Rita by the arm and guiding her up the street. "Got an objection?"

"It's all going pretty fast. What's next: the altar?"

"No altars for Buddy Dickson, I'm afraid," said Buddy. "Buddy Dickson has this thing for independence."

"The lone wolf type, huh?" asked Rita, looking up into Buddy's face.

"Oh, don't think ill of me, baby," Buddy replied. "I'm as innocent as a babe."

"Yeah, a babe raised in Vegas and educated in New Orleans."

He looked down at her and gave her a devilish little grin. "How'd you know?"

"Not too hard to figure." Rita looked up Rexford towards Little Santa Monica. "Where we going anyway?"

"Great little Italian joint right up here. Capicola like you wouldn't believe! And the spumoni! Mama Mia!" Buddy Dickson smacked his lips and smiled. It looked like it was going to be a beautiful night.

9

After dinner, Buddy Dickson took Rita White by the arm and they headed south on Bedford. "Wasn't that a sumptuous meal?" Buddy wanted to know. Rita agreed, her mushroom gnocchi was perfection and the spumoni had lived up to Buddy's praise. I was a little concerned about the price of the meal (one hundred and forty-five dollars!) but Buddy didn't seem to mind. Money was merely a means to an end for him, and the end was the ass of this beautiful woman walking by his side.

"Where are we going now?" Rita asked and Buddy said he would take her home but he had taken a taxi to Beverly Hills, being that his Mercedes was in the shop, and she said that was no problem, she could take him home, and Buddy Dickson insisted that that wasn't necessary but she countered that she wanted to and so he agreed and they headed down Bedford to a city lot. I wasn't quite sure what Buddy was thinking. Did he intend to take her to my place in West Adams, a modest house that certainly didn't seem like it befitted someone of Buddy Dickson's stature? But Buddy was confident, as always, and so I left it up to him.

When we got to the lot, Buddy took Rita into the elevator and she pushed the button for the fourth floor. On the ride up, Buddy sidled up to Rita and kissed her on the cheek. I am very awkward around women, as would be anyone whose only contact with females has been monthly visits to massage parlors, but Buddy Dickson was smooth as silk and seemed to know exactly the right moves as Rita yielded to him, even parting her lips so they could French kiss right there in the elevator. Arrived at the fourth floor, Rita said, "It's that Corolla over there," and as we walked to her car, Rita slipped the keys into Buddy's hands. Buddy Dickson opened the door for Rita White and then he and I got behind the wheel.

I have to say that Buddy Dickson was a much better driver than I am. He took the curves and handled the steering wheel like a pro, one hand on the wheel, the other around Rita White. He drove up Coldwater Canyon and I didn't know where the hell he thought he was going. It certainly wasn't to my house which was in the opposite direction. "Where do you live?" asked Rita White, and Buddy Dickson said, "Mulholland Drive," which of course was a complete surprise to me.

"You sure are sweet," said Buddy, and he smiled so suavely I didn't even recognize myself. It felt like a different face had covered my own, a face I had invented but didn't recognize. I guess this is what happens when actors really immerse themselves in their roles. The border between their selves and their characters gets mushy and mixed-up. No wonder so many actors and actresses are crazy.

"Thanks, Buddy," said Rita, returning the smile. "You're pretty sweet yourself." She leaned into Buddy and kissed him on the cheek, then stuck her tongue in his ear. Buddy squealed and laughed. "That tickles!" he cried. Rita laughed and said, "Tickling is good for you. Relaxes the nerves, gets the blood flowing."

"I didn't know that," said Buddy. He glanced at her, his look filled with a sexual energy that I knew I didn't have. "Maybe you got a lot to teach me," Buddy said. "I love to learn. And I'm a very good student."

Where was Buddy coming up with this stuff? Lines that sounded like they were straight out of a B movie from the 1950s, and yet when Buddy Dickson spoke them they didn't sound superficial or stereotypical or dumb at all, but instead they sounded smooth and cool and sexy. This certainly wasn't like me.

On my monthly visits to the Thai massage parlor, I could barely tell the girls what I wanted or ask how much certain things cost. I wasn't born with the gift of gab, but Buddy Dickson certainly had it, and in spades.

Buddy guided the Corolla up to the top of Coldwater Canyon and then took a right on Mulholland Drive. I had no idea where he was going but evidently Buddy Dickson did. The lights from Los Angeles and the San Fernando Valley sparkled down below, such a luminous display, like a million diamonds glinting and gleaming.

"Wow, it's so beautiful up here," said Rita, taking in the display of light while we twisted around the curves of Mulholland. "Must be nice living here."

"Yeah, it is," said Buddy as if he actually did live up here. And he sounded so self-assured, so confident, so smooth and calm, that I began to wonder if Buddy was right: maybe he did live up here and I just didn't know it. But wait, how could that be? Wasn't Buddy me and wasn't I Buddy? We were one and the same and yet it was obvious that we were completely different. While I was trying to puzzle this out, Buddy Dickson said, "My pad's just around the next corner. Right beyond Jack Nicholson's crib."

Crib? Pad? These weren't words I ever used but they rolled off Buddy Dickson's tongue like syrup.

"Gee, Jack Nicholson," said Rita White. "Do you know him?"

"Well, truth be told: yeah. We play pinochle every Sunday and we own a filly out at Santa Anita."

Rita White giggled. "Oh come on," she said, "that's not true."

"Should we make a pit-stop and ask Jack?" said Buddy Dickson and there was something so cool and self-assured about his manner, I even believed him while Rita White just gazed at him with the sense of appreciation and awe that comes to those who know the fortunate and the famous here in Los Angeles, the capital of the fortunate and the famous. "Wow," she said, "you're a friend of Jack's."

Buddy shrugged it off like it was no big deal and there were plenty more celebrities where that one came from. Meanwhile, I was petrified. Not only of what Buddy was saying but also by his driving, which was way too fast for me, and most especially by this girl sitting next to me, kissing me on the cheek, the smell of her perfume and the feel of her body. What was I going to do with her? Where was I taking her? I suppose Buddy Dickson knew what he was doing—it sure seemed that way—but I had no idea what was going on or where the night was headed.

Finally we rounded a big curve and Buddy Dickson pulled the car onto the shoulder.

"What are we doing?" asked Rita White.

"Just want to show you something," said Buddy Dickson, switching off the ignition. "Something very beautiful."

Buddy climbed out of the car and opened Rita White's door. We were on the Valley side of Mulholland and down below us the lights of Burbank and Pacoima and Encino and Sherman Oaks and Glendale and Granada Hills and Paramount were spread out like a big blanket of gleaming electricity. Buddy leaned on the hood of the car and gestured to the vista. "Now ain't that something," he said. I was kind of cold myself and wanted to get back in the car and go home but apparently Rita and Buddy were just fine as they leaned together and beheld the view. "It's something all right," said Rita and then Buddy looked over at her and said in that soft suave voice of his, "You're so beautiful," and Rita White blushed, a flush of crimson visible even in the darkness and then Buddy Dickson kissed her and Rita White kissed him back and then Buddy reached around and took her in his arms and even though I couldn't quite fathom how it happened, he put his tongue inside her mouth and she responded in the same way and I have to admit it felt real good even if I was scared and wanted to run.

Then Buddy guided Rita back into the car, into the back seat this time, and both of them were starting to breathe deeply. I just wanted to go home and watch late night TV but Buddy Dickson was having none of that garbage. He was here with a woman on top of Mulholland Drive with a million lights shining down below and his hunger apparently would not be denied. Once he got Rita White into the back seat of the Corolla he didn't waste any time. He had her clothes off in no time even though Rita White was starting to struggle against his advances. "No, not yet, Buddy," she said, "it's too soon," to which Buddy Dickson said, "It can't come soon enough, baby," and then he ripped off her brassiere and she screamed, "Buddy, no!" and then Buddy said, "There's no stopping me now, you bitch," and he ripped off her panties and I didn't know what to do, all I could do was look on in horror and try to get out of there but I couldn't get Buddy Dickson to move, and Rita said, "Buddy, no!" but by then it was way too late, for Buddy had entered her and he was rocking away while she whimpered below him, begging him to stop. Meanwhile, I was curled up in the corner of the passenger seat, wondering if I should call the police or just jump out of the car and run for it. Buddy heaved away and Rita moaned in such distress and then Buddy was done and he pushed Rita away.

Buddy Dickson got out of the car and lit a cigarette. I heard him mutter something, it sounded like "Stupid cunt," and I wondered what the hell was wrong with this guy. He had started out so cool, so debonair, and he had turned out so uncouth, so wrong. I might have to put his toupee away and not allow him out into the open again. Rita White slowly got out of the car. She was still half-dressed and her hair was all askew. "Wasn't that a hot time in the old town tonight, baby," said Buddy, and Rita whispered, "You bastard," and Buddy chuckled and then he said, "What's wrong, baby? You didn't like it?" and Rita White just repeated, "You bastard," and Buddy laughed and said, "A little variety might make your conversation more interesting," and for the third time Rita said, "You bastard!" only this time it was louder and after she said it she took a wild swing at Buddy Dickson but Buddy grabbed her by the wrist and threw her down on the ground.

Just then the headlights of an oncoming car came into view but Rita was lying in the dark on the far side of the Corolla and Buddy waved at the car and it swept by and went along, following its lights as it swung back and forth along Mulholland Drive and disappeared from view. "Time to go home, baby," said Buddy Dickson as Rita White rose from the ground, her dress covered in dust. "I'm going home, you piece of shit," she said. "You can walk, as far as I'm concerned."

"I don't think so, baby." He took Rita's keys out of his pocket and jingled them in the air. "'Member, I got the keys. You're just along for the fuck." I couldn't believe what Buddy Dickson was saying. This was not the way I meant for this to happen. Buddy was supposed to be a gentleman. Maybe a little too slick, maybe a little too smooth, but a gentleman nevertheless. But this wasn't a gentleman. This was something mean and nasty. I was starting to wish I'd never met Buddy Dickson. Or that he'd never returned after getting his toupee ripped off his head in the bus that day. But what could I do? Buddy Dickson had manifested himself and now he was in charge. All I could do was try and mitigate the damage. Get him home as soon as possible without causing any more damage. "Get in the car," Buddy said to Rita and Rita complied, climbing into the passenger seat. Buddy turned the engine over and we started to make our way down from Mulholland Drive.

Rita White cried the whole way down the hill. Every once

in a while she'd mutter, "Bastard, you bastard," and Buddy just smiled, only once saying, "Thanks," and I was just sitting in the back seat, wondering how this had ever happened and why Buddy Dickson was being such a creep. I had always treated women with respect, even the Asian girls at the massage parlor. I tried to do my business with them as nicely and politely as I could and I'd never been the cause of any complaints. But here was Buddy Dickson on his first date and he'd molested and assaulted and basically raped a woman. I had to get him back to the house and put him away in a drawer, never to reappear. But first I had to get through this night with no more damage.

"Where do you live, Rita darling?" Buddy Dickson asked, and there was an awful tone in his voice, sarcastic and mean, even though it was layered in a sheen of charm and concern. That thin sheen made it seem even worse, like he was making a mockery of gallantry and romance.

"West Hollywood. Right off of Santa Monica Boulevard." It sounded like Rita White could barely get the words out, she was so traumatized. I wanted to tell her it was all right, maybe take her in my arms and gently rock her, but of course Buddy Dickson was having none of that. "West Hollywood," he said again, with that cruel tone right underneath the surface of the words. "Are you a fag, Rita? Are you a fag hag? Are all your boyfriends prancing and preening little fags?" What I really wanted to do was punch Buddy Dickson right in the mouth, but I couldn't move.

"You are such a piece of shit," Rita White said, the rage in her voice almost visible.

Buddy Dickson mocked her: "Oh my goodness, is that what I am? A piece of shit?"

I sat there, silent and invisible. The car felt like it was pressing in on me, like it would fold together and crush me. I thought about reaching for the door handle and opening it and hurling myself out of the car, but what good would that do? Buddy Dickson would still be inside the car with Rita White, and then what?

"The worst piece of shit in the world," said Rita White.

"Least I got a place of honor there," said Buddy Dickson. "I am a superlative, embodied. As the worst piece of shit in the world, I shine, I am big and large and wonderful in my badness." Buddy was grinning, like everything was just a joke.

And then Rita White said something that maybe she shouldn't've, especially considering how everything turned out. "And then there's the idiotic stupid toupee of yours—who the fuck do you think you're fooling?"

Buddy didn't hesitate. The metal flashed quickly and then Buddy plunged it deep into her. Her face went blank, shocked, like she couldn't believe this was happening, which I am sure is exactly how she felt. "How do you like that, bitch?" Buddy said right into Rita's face, which was going white as her eyes went wide with the realization that she was soon to be dead.

I couldn't believe it. What had Buddy done? He had killed Rita White. He had killed Rita White just because she had insulted his rug. What kind of a monster was this? Where had he come from? Who was he?

Buddy shoved Rita White away as he whistled through his teeth. Then he softly said, in a voice that seemed to be about as close as you could come to pure evil: "Another bitch bites the dust."

I was cowering in the back seat. I couldn't move, I couldn't speak. I couldn't even breathe. But I knew I needed to get Buddy Dickson home, fast. I needed to take his clothes and burn them. Along with the toupee. Maybe that would stop him before it was too late. But wasn't it too late already?

And what should I do with Rita White? Just leave her in her

car somewhere? Dump her in a vacant lot? Take her to a police station?

No, no, I couldn't do that. They'd only throw Buddy Dickson into a cell and that wouldn't do anything to bring Rita White back to life. Besides, I needed to destroy Buddy Dickson myself. I had created him and I needed to destroy him. I felt like Jekyll and Hyde except for one big difference. Well, really two big differences. Jekyll and Hyde were connected, one animal fused through chemistry and biology. Me and Buddy Dickson didn't have anything in common: he was Buddy and I was me and no bit of chemistry or biology or physiology could connect us. And then there was the fact that Buddy Dickson was only one of the people I had created. There was Charlie McCoy and there was Frank Bunyan and I knew there were lots of other people there as well. And so even if there was a connection between me and Buddy, which I don't think there was, that link was kind of insignificant compared to the connection between Jekyll and Hyde.

Buddy drove down Coldwater Canyon with the corpse of Rita White by his side. He didn't look at her. He didn't say anything. He just drove, his demonic face lit up by the lights of the dashboard. The bloody knife was in his lap. The knife with the blood of Rita White all over it was in his lap.

At the bottom of Coldwater, there's a fire station and across the street from it there's a little park. Buddy Dickson pulled the Corolla over to the side of the road in front of the park. He checked both ways to make sure the coast was clear. Then he got out of the car and dragged Rita White across the grass to the children's area of the little park. He propped Rita White up on the slide so she was lying at the bottom of it. Then he looked at his handiwork and smiled and moved back to the car.

I just sat there. I couldn't believe this was happening. What had Buddy Dickson done? What had I done? But I hadn't done anything. True, I had dressed up as Buddy Dickson. True, I had given him a knife. But the knife was supposed to be for self-defense, that's all, honestly. I had never intended it to be used like this. Now the blood of Rita White was smeared all over it and I didn't know what to do. But Buddy Dickson did. He threw the knife out the window at La Brea and Sunset. The sound of it landing on the street was haunting and strange, a sound I heard over and over and can still hear echoing in my brain today.

Buddy Dickson dumped Rita White's Corolla near the corner of La Brea and Venice and then took the 33 home. I was with him on the bus. I gazed out the window. I could see Buddy Dickson with me in the reflection on the window. He was smiling and humming a tune. I was not.

10

The fire was burning in the sink. It was burning up Buddy Dickson's clothes. Rita White's blood was on the clothes, a smear across the right arm of Buddy's coat, the arm with the hand that had thrust the knife into the heart of Rita White. The last thing to go was Buddy Dickson's toupee, that wig that had brought so much trouble to me and Buddy and Rita White. The black hair gleamed with light as it burned. It smelled like burning plastic, a weird scent that almost hurt the nose.

When it was all gone, a thin sheet of ashes was left in the sink. I thought about gathering them together and burying them in the backyard but then I decided just to wash them down the sink. Buddy didn't deserve a burial and leaving any sort of trace of Buddy around maybe wasn't such a good idea. Better to get rid of him completely.

After the last trace of ashes had drained into the sink, I stood there for a moment, contemplating everything and wondering what to do. I thought about giving up the whole thing of putting on costumes and disguises and roaming the city streets. But I couldn't do it. It was the one thing in my life I had. What was I supposed to do? Just return to being a zero? I couldn't face it, the anonymity, the loneliness, the pain. Besides, it wasn't the disguises and the costumes that were wrong; it was Buddy Dickson. Something about Buddy was beyond repair. He was flawed from the very get-go. I'd just have to be more careful. Really examine each person before I took them out on the streets. And then be ready for any contingency so that I didn't freeze up like I had with Buddy Dickson and Rita White. Yes, I just needed to get my routine down right and then everything would run smoothly. No more rapes, no more murders. Not even any petty crimes or misdemeanors would be tolerated. I wouldn't even jaywalk. I wouldn't even think bad thoughts. Everything would be cool.

But there was something else happening as well. Something which I couldn't admit to myself at the time. Something I would only recognize much later after I had killed a few more people. And then, of course, it was too late.

11

I took a break for about a week and hardly even left the house. I kept looking for a mention of Rita White in the paper or on the nightly news but there was nothing. I guess one person's death didn't warrant much attention, not here in L.A., where hundreds of people are killed every year.

But after about ten days or so of lying low, I started getting antsy. I needed to be sure about what I was doing though. I couldn't afford another mistake. So I decided to be a woman. I figured women get in a lot less trouble than men and are basically much more peaceful. A woman wouldn't go and knife someone in the heart just because they figured out she was wearing a wig. A women would take it all in stride and not get upset over such small tomatoes.

I went and bought a dress, hoping that my guess at the size would be right as I certainly wasn't going to try the thing on. Then I got some high heels, a black wig and some makeup. I was a little embarrassed about getting all this stuff but I just made up a story about a sister coming to town and the clerks all smiled. They didn't really care, as long as they made a sale.

I worked on putting this person together for two weeks. Her name was Glenda McPhee and she was a receptionist in a law office. She was a widow, her husband's name was Fred, and she was from Winnemucca, Nevada. She was a good cook and liked to dance. She had lived in Los Angeles since 1977 and all of her family were dead except for one aunt who lived in Buffalo. Her hobbies were stitchery, listening to the baseball games on the radio, and birding. I even got a couple of books on birds from the library and memorized some of them, like the magpie and the sparrow and the meadowlark. It was a nice project and almost took my mind off of what had happened to Rita White. But I kept seeing the stillness of that face and the blood running out from between her ribs. I was glad I had punished Buddy Dickson, as there was something so basically wrong about him. But now he was dead, just like Rita, and so everything seemed like it had been taken care of, fair and square.

It took me quite a while to find any sort of stability in those high heels. How women stand these things is beyond me. But finally I got it after walking up and down my hallway about a thousand and one times. I had to practice the makeup a lot too but I found some good places on the Internet which were very helpful. The Internet itself is such a godsend. In the old days, I would have had to go out in public to take a makeup class and of course I couldn't've done that. Now you could do everything in the privacy of your own home and that made me feel nice and safe and secure.

Finally I was ready to take Glenda McPhee out on the streets. I wanted to try something real simple first so we just went out for a cup of coffee. There's a Starbucks at Washington and Crenshaw and Glenda got a tall iced coffee there. The people at the counter didn't seem to notice anything weird about Glenda even though she was six foot two and weighed about one eighty. Just another customer, as far as they were concerned.

One funny thing did happen at Starbucks. A guy flirted with Glenda. At least I think he was flirting. What he did was he came over to my table and asked me what I was drinking. He was an Asian guy, maybe fifty, kind of handsome and fit, a mustache, wearing a Dodgers shirt, number forty-two, Jackie Robinson. I told him what I was drinking and he asked me if I wanted another.

I told him I was fine thank you, and then he asked me if I came to this Starbucks very often. I said pretty often and then he smiled and said that maybe he'd see me again. And then he left and went back to his table where he was sitting alone, one of those blended drinks with whipped cream in front of him. I smiled at him, he smiled back, and that was that.

Back home, I was very pleased with the expedition. Basically, nothing had happened, which was exactly the way I had wanted it to go. Oh sure, there were a few people on the bus who had stared at this big white lady walking down the aisle, and yes, that guy in Starbucks had tried to pick me up or something, but there was nothing wrong with all of that. In fact, it only demonstrated that everything went fine, as the people in the bus hadn't done anything besides look and the guy at Starbucks had only talked to me, so that these things were like marks of everything being normal, given that I was a woman and six feet two, one hundred eighty pounds.

The next thing I did with Glenda was take her to Monterrey Park for dim sum. We went to the Elite on Atlantic Boulevard. Again, nothing happened, just ordered from the carts and paid my fare. None of the customers in the place, pretty much all of whom were Asian and I guess Chinese, even glanced at me except for one little boy, maybe five or six years old, who cried out loudly, "That's a big girl, Mommy! Look at her!" but his mother shushed him up real quickly and then there was nothing else.

Waiting for the bus back home from Monterrey Park, I thought about my next move. Everything seemed to be going smoothly with Glenda and maybe I just could proceed along with her and see where it would take me. I have to admit, I really enjoyed being a girl. I felt like I had entered some secret world, and of course in many ways I had. I did my best to act like a woman too, basing everything on the movie stars I had watched as a kid, actresses like Kim Novak and Natalie Wood and Ann Margaret and even Marilyn Monroe and of course all the women in the James Bond movies, you know, like Pussy Galore. They had all looked like they were so comfortable in their bodies, like they just carried the female within them without a thought. I mean, sure, maybe they thought about it a lot, obviously they must have, what with all the make-up and the costumes and the way they walked and talked and everything, but they made it seem like all of this just came along naturally, with no to-do about it. Like they were encased within femininity and they were revealing it to the world, moment by moment. I'm not sure if I'm getting it quite right, as it's a pretty elusive thing I'm trying to describe, but maybe you know what I mean. A real woman is a real woman without ever showing what it takes to be a real woman. And that's what I was trying to do. Which is pretty hard to pull off, if you're a guy and even if you're a woman. But, like I said, I think I did at least a passable job of it, given that no one had made any weird comments or anything, that is, except for that kid in the dim sum place, and that doesn't really count because he was just a kid.

The high heels were killing me though. I don't know how women ever get used to this. The pain in my heels and my toes and my arches and just about everywhere was unbelievable. Every man should be made to wear them for one day just to see what they are like. There should be a monument on The Mall in Washington D.C. dedicated to the pain women have undergone due to these monstrous things.

As I took the bus home, I started noticing something that was kind of weird but which I really should have expected all along. My feelings were different. I was noticing things that I had never noticed before. Like the texture of things were so much easier to feel and the colors of things were so much more, well, colorful.

As a woman I was seeing so much more and even hearing things which I had never heard before. It was like all my senses had opened up into a new and different level, a level closer to the actuality of things. Or at least that's the way it seemed to me and I'm pretty sure that was what was actually happening. Even the slightest movement or gesture of the other passengers on the bus were gigantic. The whole world seemed to have been magnified and telescoped, like everything was suddenly close, so close it almost hurt. It was like I had never sensed anything before and now everything was rushing at me in a flood or an avalanche or something. When the bus lurched, I lurched too. When a kid on the bus turned his music up on his I-phone, every note penetrated my skull. The grime and grit on the floor of the bus were like huge marks that jumped into my eyes. And the smells in the bus were like visible things, things that rose up and soared into my nose, almost making me gag. So this was what it was like for a woman! No wonder they were moody. If I'd had to withstand this kind of barrage every moment of my life, I'd be pretty damn moody too.

When the bus came to my stop, I stepped off to the curb, those heels making all my movements a little wobbly. Then I walked down Wilton Place to my house. And this is when it happened. What I had feared for quite a while. That one of my neighbors would spot me and figure out what was going on or at least know that something was going on.

I was just walking up the street, minding my own business, when this young Mexican kid from the apartment building next door rides by on his bike. He doesn't say anything but I'm pretty sure he recognized me cause he wheeled back around and passed me again, looking at me real close. But then, so what? People in this neighborhood generally leave one another alone. That is, unless there's a crime with a victim involved, or maybe drug-dealing. It's just an unwritten code. Live and let live. There's a lot of undocumented people and a lot of people who have been in and out of jail, so it's just policy not to dig into other people's stuff. So that kid probably wouldn't even tell his parents or his friends. That is, if he did recognize me, which I wasn't even sure he had. So it didn't worry me too much. Everyone in the neighborhood most likely already thought I was weird, a lonely old white man living by himself in a neighborhood full of Latinos and black people, so what was a little more weirdness piled on top of that?

I went inside my house and got out of Glenda's clothes. I was all tuckered out from being a woman all day, those heels and everything, and so I grabbed a beer and watched some TV for a while. I surfed the channels but the only thing worth watching was something TCM had on. It was Dirk Bogarde in a thing called *Victim*, where he plays a lawyer going to battle against some blackmailers who are threatening to expose men for being gay, Bogarde himself being gay in the film. This got me to thinking about homosexuality and what it might be like to be gay. Was it anything like being a woman? Or was it just like being a guy except you were attracted to men? Me, I had never had a homosexual experience. Heck, I had hardly even had any heterosexual experiences, especially if my monthly visits to the Thai massage parlor got subtracted from the list.

I decided I was going to be Benny Monger. A gay bank manager who lived alone with his mother. Wait—no no no, he didn't live alone with his mother—that's too much of a cliché. A gay man who lived alone. Yes, that's better. Smart, intelligent, a good dresser. Maybe a mustache? Maybe a beard? No, no facial hair, too much of a hassle to put on and take off, and getting it right isn't that easy either. I'd have to buy a few things, as my clothes weren't stylish enough for a gay guy. But it wouldn't take that much. I just needed one costume and that would be that.

Meanwhile, I'd watch some movies that featured gay characters, you know, like *Philadelphia* and *Broke Back Mountain* and *The Dallas Buyer's Club*, just to get the feeling down and everything.

So I'd give Glenda McPhee a little rest and take Benny Monger out on the street. That was the plan. And a good one too, I thought. At least at the time.

The next day I went shopping at The Grove and got everything I needed. Me, I hate to go shopping, I just order from catalogues, but I figured that gay people like to shop, which I suppose is a stereotype, but maybe there's some truth to it anyway. So I tried to have a great time, trying on this and that, looking at myself in the mirror, chatting up the clerks. Finally, I got everything I wanted and took it home, the bags almost too much for me to take on the bus, but I made it, clutching everything together like I was going to a Christmas party with a whole bunch of presents in my arms. When I got home, I tried everything on and I was really pleased. I didn't buy anything fancy or flamboyant, just sharp stuff that fit nice on me. Creased white Gap slacks, a J. Crew shirt and Mephisto shoes, which were the only thing I got that was kind of pricey, but I've always had a soft spot for shoes, as a good pair can make all the difference between a nice comfy day and one straight from hell. I also picked up a purse for Glenda at Nordstrom's, a big black bulky thing which I told the clerk was a birthday present for my Aunt Norma. He could have cared less, I'm sure, but for some reason I felt like a cover story was necessary for a man purchasing a purse.

I worked on Benny Monger's voice that night, pitching it a little bit higher than mine and letting him say words that I usually didn't say. Words like "Impossible" and "Appreciate" and "Surcharge." Then I got on the computer and surfed through some gay porn sites to see if I could work up an interest. It didn't really work but maybe that's because I've never liked any kind of porn, even straight stuff. So I didn't worry about this too much. Then I looked at some male models on the Internet, young blonde guys wearing swim suits, and moody-looking dark-skinned guys in Italian suits. I could see that these guys were strikingly handsome, sure, but I wasn't super attracted or anything. But maybe that was all right. After all, I was just pretending to be gay; I wasn't actually going to be gay, and there is a big difference, right?

The next day I got Benny Monger on and went over to Western to catch the bus up to Santa Monica Boulevard. I had decided to take him out to lunch somewhere in West Hollywood and see how it went. I ended up at a nice Mexican place near the Blue Whale, eating fish tacos and just sort of trying to see everything through Benny Monger's eyes. I smiled at the waiter in the way I thought a gay guy might do it, kind of flirtatious and suggestive, I guess. And it wasn't that hard to do because the guy was actually pretty nice-looking, maybe thirty, "Fred," his name-tag said, fit, black hair, sort of Latin-looking, like maybe he was a Mexican or a Cuban or something. He smiled back at me but I couldn't tell if he was flirting too or just playing the part of a waiter and hoping for a good tip. Maybe I'd been too friendly, so I backed off and didn't say too much for the rest of the meal, but I did leave a big tip, five dollars for a twelve-dollar lunch. I wanted him to remember me. Why, I wasn't quite sure. Maybe I was overcompensating, trying to prove that I was gay by being really gay. Or maybe Benny Monger was just a real generous guy.

After lunch, I strolled the streets and went into a shop and bought a shirt. No one overreacted to me or did anything weird. Which, as always, was half the battle. As long as people didn't look at me funny I figured I had been successful in whatever disguise I was wearing. But again, as I've said before, it's a little hard to tell what people are really thinking, as no one holds their cards too open or lets you know what's on their mind, especially service workers like store clerks and waiters and such, being as it's their job to be nice to everyone, no matter how weird the person might be, even if it's some odd-looking retired guy getting dressed up in costumes as a hobby.

But is that what this was? A hobby? If it was a hobby, it sure was an odd one. I'd never heard of anyone else doing anything like this. Hobbies were supposed to be like stamp collecting and hiking and golf and stuff like that. It wasn't dressing up like Glenda McPhee in high heels and going out for dim sum in Monterey Park. And it wasn't like dressing up like Benny Monger and flirting with a waiter named Fred at a Mexican restaurant next to the Blue Whale. And it sure as hell wasn't dressing up like a Vegas card shark and raping and killing a woman.

Buddy Dickson, Buddy Dickson. What a mistake that had been. Nothing like that could ever happen again.

And of course nothing like that ever did happen again. But worse things did…much worse. But I have to go in order. Tell things like they happened. One event after another. Like a real story. Cause it is a real story. One with costumes and disguises and rape and murder.

12

The next morning when I woke up I was thinking of Fred. That was weird. Why would I be thinking about him? Okay, he was young and handsome and I had flirted with him at the taco place, but I was straight and he seemed to be gay, so what did we have in common? Maybe there was something paternal about how I felt about Fred, maybe I was just filling a void 'cause I had never had the chance to be a dad and he was about the age a son of mine would be if I'd ever had one, a son, that is.

I really didn't want to go back to the restaurant right after the day I'd been there. That seemed like too much, like maybe I was crazy or something. Or at least a big flirt. Or so horny I couldn't resist. Or so smitten with Fred I couldn't keep away. Or all of those things combined. And I didn't want to give the impression of any of those things. Plus, maybe it was a little too risky, taking Benny Monger right back to the exact same place he had been the day before. Better to let it sit for a day or two. Still, I couldn't ignore this feeling inside, kind of like a compulsion or something, that wanted to take me back to West Hollywood and a waiter named Fred.

But in the end I fought it off and went with Glenda McPhee instead. It just felt so much safer to be a woman than a gay guy. Somehow I understood her better. Or at least I thought I did. Though, given what happened that day, maybe I didn't understand her at all .

Once dressed and all made up, I got on the Washington Boulevard bus and headed downtown. As the bus pitched and swayed and rolled forward, I noticed something very strange. It was like the bus was pitching and swaying and rolling right under me and sending waves of energy up my body right into my thighs and my hips and my waist. And then I started to feel like these surges of energy were rolling right up into my sexual organs except that my sexual organs didn't feel like a man's at all. It was like my testicles and my penis had disappeared and had been replaced by a vagina. I know that sounds kind of crazy but that's what it felt like. I mean I was wearing a bra and panties and high heels and I did have rouge and lipstick on, so maybe it's not weird at all that I felt this way but still it felt pretty weird. Because even while it was happening I was trying to stop it from happening, but I couldn't stop it from happening because I was enjoying what was happening so much. And that last thing is really hard to acknowledge, but anyway there it is: I felt like I had a real vagina inside my panties and that every last little motion of the bus was rushing up into it and titillating me. My penis got hard and now I was really confused. Did I have a penis or a vagina? Or both? Or did my penis get so hard just because it was rubbing up against my panties? I'm not sure because all I knew was that I wished I was back in my house so I could hide this erection that would not let up. I had Glenda's purse parked right on my lap so no one could see my boner, but that didn't matter as I felt like everyone could see it, and that was the only thing they were looking at, this erection bursting up through my panties as the bus roared down Washington Boulevard bound for downtown L.A.

At Western Avenue, an older black gentleman sat next to Glenda McPhee. I hoped his presence would get my dick in order, that it would subside and get back to normal. But no such thing happened and in fact it even got bigger, as if I was attracted to this bald black man in a Kobe tee shirt and blue jeans. I turned away from him and looked out the window, expecting that maybe the sights of buildings and cars would empty my mind of sexual yearnings and drive that boner back into its place. But that didn't work either, as it was the actual grind and motion of the bus that was turning on my penis-vagina, as if every quiver and shiver of the motor and the axle were shooting up my spine and filling Glenda's member with blood.

"You're sure a tall glass of water, sister."

I couldn't even quite fathom where this voice was coming from. I turned and looked at the black man sitting next to me, as if this might possibly be the source of those words which I couldn't connect together into anything meaningful or whole. He was smiling at me so I figured it was him who had said whatever it was he had said.

"What?" I asked.

"Are you a player?"

"A player"? What could that possibly mean? Like a basketball player? Or that I played the horses? Or did he mean did I…

"What?" was all I could say again, as that one word seemed to define me. And then I happily noticed that my erection seemed to be subsiding, which was certainly good news.

"Come on, baby. Don't play dumb," he said and then he put his hand on my thigh. "I was just hoping maybe we could—you know."

"No, I don't know," and now I was surprised because it seemed to me that my voice had the feel of some alarmed spinster from a 1950s-era movie. Like maybe I needed a fan to go along with my voice and then I would hit this fresh lout on the head with it and show him who was boss and whose virtue could not be violated.

"Oh fuck, baby," said the man, shaking his head. "Come on, you come out splayed out like that in public with the high heels on and the lipstick and everything, and then you want to go and imagine you're not going to get some guy coming on to you, you gotta be motherfucking crazy."

I had the impulse to stand up and move to another seat but I didn't want to cause more of a scene than had already started to develop, because people were starting to turn and stare at me and this black man who was swearing at me, his voice getting louder and louder. I even thought the bus driver was glancing in his mirror to check out what was going on before something exploded out of control. So I just said, "Please," hoping that one word might placate this guy and shut him the hell up.

But he had other plans. "Now listen, honey," he said, "you can either get up and go with me or you can have this shiv run up into your heart." I felt something sharp in my side. I looked down. There was a short but very lethal-looking blade in the man's right hand and the point was poking into my ribs. "Now what we're going to do, baby, is get off the bus at the next stop, real slow and real comfy. Okay?" His voice had gone low and sort of gentle in a real creepy way. People turned away, thinking everything was okay. The bus driver was just looking at the road ahead.

Well, what choice did I have? "Okay." But at least my erection had completely gone away: that much was good.

"That's a nice girl."

The bus pulled over at New England Street and me and the black man got out of the bus. "Turn on down there," he said.

I obeyed and we walked past a recycling center and a few small houses. Up ahead was the Santa Monica Freeway, the din of cars sounding out continuously as they cruised the highway.

"Up here," he said, indicating a kind of empty space underneath the freeway, with dirt below and the eight lanes of the 10 up above. We had to climb up a dirt bank to get there and my high heels did not make this an easy task, as they kept torquing my ankles this way and that. There was a dirty blanket in there and some empty tin cans and a shopping cart tipped over on its side. "Lie down," the man ordered, and I did as I was told, as who wouldn't with the point of a blade poking into their back. I lay down on the dirty blanket and the black man stood over me, the knife in his hand. "You look delicious, baby," he said, lying down next to me.

I didn't know what to do. Where was this going? And what would this madman do once he found out he was dealing with a man and not a woman? But maybe he already knew I was a man and didn't care, or even liked it. Maybe that was this guy's thing and I was exactly what he wanted. But any way you looked at it, I didn't want to be there. What was I supposed to do? Maybe try and grab the knife when the guy got all worked up and excited, that is, if he ever did get all worked up and excited. But if I did that and it didn't work out, he might shove the knife right into me and turn the blade, ending my life just when I was starting to really enjoy it.

"Take off your skirt, honey," the man ordered and I complied, though I did it with the clumsiness of a man who has not worn a skirt too often, which of course was exactly the situation I found myself in. I tossed it to the side and the black skirt rolled into the dust. Meanwhile, the din from the freeway was sounding out overhead, a gigantic roar that played along with everything we were doing. I kept thinking that thousands of people were zooming by and if only one could see down there, they might call the police and rescue me from this weird escapade. Yet did I really want some police officers questioning me in my dress and high heels?

The man lay on top of me and started rubbing around and groaning, the knife still tilted up and ready to go. "Oh baby, you are one big bundle of joy."

That's when it happened. He reached for what he thought

would be a vagina and felt a penis instead. "You bitch!" he cried. "You're a goddamn motherfuckin' man, not a goddamn motherfuckin' woman!" He leaned back, staring into my eyes with a frightening combination of disbelief, wonder, and absolute anger. "Why'd you do this to me?!"

"I didn't do anything to you," I said, trying to reassure the man before he did anything rash.

"I'm cutting that cock off for you, bitch! Then you won't have to worry about nothing and you'll never lead another goddamn stupid motherfucker down the wrong motherfuckin' street!"

He grabbed my penis with his left hand and lowered the knife with his right hand down to the shaft of my penis. I had to do something and fast, otherwise I'd be dickless, castrated, emasculated and cut to pieces. My hands went for the knife, naturally, and I grabbed his wrist with both my hands and managed to push the knife away and pin his hand down to the dirt. I got aboard the man, throwing all my weight against him, as I outweighed him by a good thirty or forty pounds.

"You fuckin' bitch, you ain't getting away with this," the black man said in a kind of a hissing voice through compressed lips. Suddenly, he jerked himself out from under me and flipped himself over on top of me. I still had his wrist in a clamp, however, but I didn't know for how long as he seemed to have so much adrenalin running through him that I wasn't sure I could keep that knife away from me. Still, if I didn't want to die or at least have my penis cut off, I had to hang on.

I gave it everything I had and flipped him over so that I was back on top. Then I pounded down my right hand and knocked the knife out of his grip. As soon as this happened, I put my hands around his throat and started squeezing with all my might. He started gasping and staring up at me with these huge bulging eyes like they were about to burst out of his face. Then I got my hands on his windpipe, I could feel it there right under his skin, and I pressed down as hard as I could. I felt something busting and collapsing and giving way. The black man made one last rattling gasp and then the life went out of him and his eyes were just hollow holes, empty and dead.

I couldn't move for a long time, that's how I exhausted I was. I just lay on top of the dead man and tried to catch my breath. I pulled on my panties and my skirt and wiped the dust off them as best as I could. Then, staggering and breathing hard, I rose and looked down at him. His head was cocked to one side and his eyes were wide open. His tongue was halfway out of his mouth and his clothes were all dirty from the fight. Just to make sure, I checked for his pulse and listened to his heart but there was nothing. I had killed him. He lay there, dead in the dirt, and I was the one who had killed him. I looked at my hands as if I might see some evidence on them but there was nothing. They were just like they always had been. The roar of the vehicles moving above on the Santa Monica Freeway made for a weird counterpoint to me and the dead man. We weren't making any noise and they were making all this noise. Yet nobody driving those cars and buses and trucks knew what was here below them. A dead black man and me in a dress with an invisible stain from the dead man's throat.

I looked around, making sure no one was there. Then I closed the man's eyes and covered him with a torn blanket that was bunched up next to some weeds. I took one last look at the dead man, straightened my skirt and then walked back down to New England Street. As I walked up to the bus stop, something very strange occurred. I began to feel very good. As a matter of fact, I started to feel a sense of peace and a feeling of joy that I had never even imagined could be felt by anybody, let alone me, Lloyd Stollman, loner, retired DMV worker, the man with the camera alone in the cubicle. It wasn't just that I had survived the battle with the would-be rapist; it was that I had killed him. And it didn't matter that it was him in particular. It was just that I had killed and I had enjoyed it. Enjoyed it? I had loved it! The power of my hands, the life rushing out of him, the excitement of it all went way beyond anything I had ever experienced. Not that I had experienced that much, but this was really something.

I had killed someone and I had enjoyed it. I wondered who would be next. Then I got in the bus and rode home. No one bothered me at all.

13

Yet I had enough sense to know that I had to lie low, take my time, pace myself. I searched for news of the dead man in the newspapers and on TV, but I couldn't find anything. Well, after all, if nothing was said about the passing of Rita White, a white woman stabbed in the heart and dumped in a park in Beverly Hills, nothing was going to be said about a black man strangled underneath the Santa Monica Freeway. And that wasn't being racist, that was just a statement of fact. Besides, what was one murder more or less in Los Angeles, when so many murders happened here? If it was a small city like Toledo or Wichita or maybe even Seattle, then, sure, it probably would have made the news, but not here in L.A. And so murder protected me, burying my murders in the overwhelming number of them in this strange and mysterious city. Or so I thought.

So I took a few weeks off and just did me, going on errands, seeing a few movies at the Arclight, visiting the Greek Observatory, taking the bus to San Diego for a couple of nights, just for the heck of it.

Actually, that's not one hundred percent true, as I did develop some new people, or characters or whatever you want to call them. James Bussey was a janitor, wore black spectacles, crisply ironed work slacks, a shirt with his name stitched into it. Stanford Madison was a rich guy, a playboy and a drunk, liked to chase the girls. And then there was Stanley Smith, a community college math professor, very straight and narrow during the day, but a big porno fan at night. I didn't take any of these out on the street, but I worked on them, developing their voices and trying out different gaits and gestures until I got the right combination that seemed to match.

I did dress up as Glenda McPhee one night. I just wanted to see what it felt like. Much as I hate to admit it, the feel of those panties against my cock was really something. Instantly, I got an erection and I pulled my penis out of the confines of the panties and started stroking. But even though I was dressed up as a female and had all the make-up on and everything, I still thought of women while I was masturbating, even if I tried to think about men. Which made me think that I was so straight nothing could ever change it, not even wearing panties, lipstick and rouge. But maybe I'm just all mixed up and have no idea of who I am. Still, when Glenda finished her jacking-off session, it was with the thought of one of the girls at the Thai massage place in her head and not of any man. When I wiped myself off and took off Glenda's clothes, I stood there naked in the room for a moment, staring down at my penis.

After that, I put away Glenda's clothes, thinking I wouldn't be her for a while. She was really mixing me up too much. The way wearing her panties aroused her wasn't healthy. Or at least I didn't think it was healthy. I guess she scared me. Plus, she had killed a man. Sure, it was in self-defense, the guy's knife about to cut off her dick and everything, but, still, she had blood on her hands.

Yet I couldn't shake the feeling I'd had after killing the man; I had liked it. Liked it? Hell, let's be honest here, it's just you and me talking. I loved it. There was something about the sense of power that had run through me while my hands were throttling that man's life out of him that gave me a thrill. But of course the thought of me liking that also scared the hell out of me. Two of my characters had already killed people.

Maybe I should have just put this game away and forgotten about Charlie McCoy and Buddy Dickson and Glenda McPhee and all the rest of them. But I couldn't do that. This was the most exciting thing that had ever happened to me in my life. I had worked in the Culver City DMV for twenty-five years, mindlessly snapping photos of people, and now something was finally happening to me, something mysterious and puzzling and beautiful. Creating these characters had given me purpose and it had gone a long way to erasing all the years of mediocrity in which I had lived. Lived? Hell, that wasn't living. That was merely existing or, even worse, subsisting. Only now was I truly alive and I couldn't kill the thing that had brought me to life. It was impossible.

Still, I knew I had to be careful, take it slow and easy, not push the limits too recklessly. I decided to go back to my beginnings and take Charlie McCoy out for an excursion. The cowboy had always been good to me and he'd been my first creation, so how could I go wrong with him?

Charlie and I decided to go downtown. So we took the Purple Line to Pershing Square and then walked up Hill Street to Grand Central Market to have lunch. I've always loved this joint and so has Charlie. The food there is great and there're so many different types of people. Plus the openness of the place, its combination of being kind of funky and kind of elegant makes it real special. I got my usual, fish tacos. Then I found a place to sit and was just sitting there, minding my own business, when a little Mexican kid ran up to me, pulled an imaginary gun out of his pocket and started blasting away at me. "Pow pow," he said, "you're dead, mister."

I feigned getting hit in the heart, grabbing my chest with my hands and leaning back as if he'd really nailed me. "You got me," I said.

"And now I'm gonna hang you," said the kid, smiling devilishly.

"Wasn't shooting me to death enough?" I asked, a little taken aback by this kid's bloodthirstiness.

"No way," said the kid. "You're a bad man and you have to pay."

"What did I do?" Now the kid was making me real uneasy. It was almost as if he knew about the two murders, the one that Buddy Dickson had done and the other one that Glenda McPhee had done. What was with this little kid anyway?

"You shot my grandfather in Laredo," he said. "And then you knifed my brother in the heart down in Abilene."

"But that was self-defense," I said, the black man's throat flashing into view. "At least that's what the jury said."

"Maybe they did," he said and now there was definitely something really evil starting to come over his face, a sharpness or a brutality. Was this kid an emissary of the devil or something? "But I am the executioner and I say you must die." And then he took the pointer finger of his right hand and put it against my temple and killed me. "Bang bang," he said. "Now you're dead, hombre." He leaned back and smiled like he was real pleased with himself, the good, solid work of the executioner. "Go to Hell."

I looked at this kid, hard. The game had quickly turned sour, real sour, real quick.

"What's wrong, mister?" he asked. "Don't you like Hell?"

I was just about to say something to this kid when a hand reached out and grabbed him. "Chico, what are you doing?"

"Aw, mom, we're just playing. He killed two people and I was taking care of his sins." He looked at me with what I swear was an evil little twinkle. "Ain't that right, mister?"

"Uh, yeah…sure."

The kid's mother apologized and I said there was nothing to apologize for, that she had a fine little boy, and then she turned away with her hand still clamped on the boy's wrist and they disappeared into the crowd, but not before the boy gave me one last look, a mean sharp-edged look that actually sent a chill up my spine, and then he cried out, `So long, cowboy,' and then I couldn't see him anymore, what with all the bodies and the food stands and everyone walking to and fro.

I hadn't finished my tacos but I wasn't hungry anymore. That kid had robbed me of my appetite. Was my guilt that easy to see? Was I wearing it on my skin like the Stetson on my head? Would the police be able to see it as easily as the little kid?

But wait a second. My thinking was all messed up. I was Charlie McCoy. The ones who had done the murdering were Buddy Dickson and Glenda McPhee, not me. I had done nothing wrong. I was just a two-bit cowboy roaming the plains. I was just a cowpoke on an adventure. I hadn't done nothing wrong, so how could they see anything in my face? The kid was just a kid. He didn't know anything at all. He was just playing around. I had to get a hold of my self. I couldn't get panicked, especially by a little Mexican kid who didn't know anything about anything.

Still, there was something about that kid that was creepy. He seemed to have some sort of secret information or knowledge, like he had been present when Buddy and Glenda had gone and done what they went and did and now he was returning to tell the tale. But that was horseshit. That kid couldn't've known anything. He was just a kid. Maybe he was creepy and weird, but he was still just a kid.

I was walking up Broadway by now, round about Fifth Street, where all the Latino street vendors spread out their wares on the sidewalks and the old movie houses stand empty, though some of them are emporiums selling all kinds of cheap Mexican crap. I turned east on Sixth Street and headed into skid row. I wasn't sure why I was going this way but this was the way I was going, so I just kept on going as if this was the way to go. As I moved forward across Spring and Main, more and more homeless people were out on the streets, pushing their shopping carts, ragged clothing, hands and faces smeared with dirt, some of them mumbling to themselves, others shouting out loud for all the world to hear. Here were the dregs of society, the debris left to drift on its own, the garbage, the living carcasses, the remainders when nothing else remained.

Charlie McCoy walked through them. Charlie McCoy witnessed their pain. Charlie McCoy was a cowboy with a heart. Charlie McCoy wished he could have ridden out on the plain and killed a bunch of buffalo so he could skin them and butcher them into nice big chunks and then feed the people on the streets. Charlie McCoy would never have let this situation fester if he had been sheriff. Charlie McCoy would have deputized the entire population and they would have made sure that no one was hungry or thirsty or lacked shelter or any of the other basic necessities of life. That was because Charlie McCoy understood suffering. He understood pain. He understood an empty belly and a long ride across enemy territory.

When a battered-looking black woman at Sixth and Main asked for spare change, I took out my wallet and gave her a five. It was worth it to see that bright smile flash for an instant on that weary face, and then she said, "Thanks, Mister," and she turned and walked away. It made Charlie McCoy feel good and he and I wished that we had five hundred dollars in ones and fives; I would have given away the whole thing and then ridden off into the sunset on Charlie McCoy's gray mare. But he only had three fives left and a couple of ones. He handed out two of the fives and all the ones by the time he got to Gladys Park, which is pretty much right in the heart of skid row. It really isn't much of a park, just a basketball court and a few benches and a worn patch of grass. No one ever goes there except homeless people and pigeons. And now of course here I was, Charlie McCoy, with that one five burning a hole in my pocket and my status as a good Samaritan standing pretty darn high, at least in my own eyes, at least in the eyes of Charlie McCoy.

"You got a nickel?" someone coming up on Charlie's right asked. This was exactly what me and Charlie McCoy were looking for. Charlie turned and, grinning, surveyed the man who had asked for the handout. He was a scruffy young white guy with wild hair and whiskers and a t-shirt that read "The Saints of Prosperity" on it and blue jeans that looked like they had been dunked in a barrel of rat shit. The man stank too, the aroma of urine lifting off him and heading directly into Charlie's nose. But I didn't care. I was Charlie McCoy and Charlie McCoy had smelled a whole lot worse things in his travels through the West. He had smelled the dead flesh of horses and the stink of a man rotting in the sun. This was nothing to him. I smiled and said to the scruffy youngster, "I think I can do better than that," and then I pulled out my wallet and handed him the five.

The kid stared at the bill as if he wasn't sure what it was. Like it was something foreign, an object brought back from Mars. Finally he said, "Wow, man, thanks," and he folded up the five-dollar bill carefully and slipped it into the side pocket of his ripped-up jeans. "Who are you, Mister?" he asked, as if trying to slot me into some pre-existing category, or as if he couldn't quite figure out what the hell I was doing in Gladys Park, what with the Stetson and the cowboy duds and the mustache and everything. "I ain't never seen you around here before."

"That's 'cause I ain't never been here before." Technically, that was true. I had been to Gladys Park before, but Charlie McCoy had never been there. "I'm Charlie McCoy. I'm a cowboy." I grinned and indicated my cowboy hat. "As you can see."

"Yeah, I seen you're a cowboy. There ain't too many of them around no more." There was something sad in the young man's voice, a sense of defeat or an ache or a pain or something. "They've all gone and disappeared. Like into the sunset or something." He said this quietly and softly and the sense of something forlorn and something all woebegone in him increased. I almost thought he was going to cry. "Me, I'm a dying breed as well."

"And what are you?" I asked.

"Me, I'm an anarcho-syndicalist." The young man looked up into the sky, as if his answer and his identification had come from up there on high.

"What's that, exactly?" me and Charlie McCoy asked.

"Well, I'm like a Wobbly."

"You mean you wobble a lot?" The anarcho-syndicalist laughed and that made me and Charlie McCoy laugh along with him, laughter being contagious and all. "You look pretty steady to me," I added.

That remark made the young man laugh even louder, he actually doubled up with it, and I went along with him, me and Charlie laughing loud too. In fact, we were all laughing so much some of other people in the park began to glance over at us, like what the hell could be so funny with this wire-haired crazy young man and the cowboy in the middle of skid row. Charlie and I respected them, their troubles and hardships and everything, so we got quiet very quickly, but the anarcho-syndicalist kept laughing for a good while longer till he finally calmed down enough to remember what we were talking about and then said, "The Wobblies were American revolutionaries who believed in freedom and dignity for the working man and woman. They rode the rails and led strikes in mining and logging camps and other places all over the country from Massachusetts to the state of Washington. They believed in one big union for everybody."

"Us cowboys don't need unions. We ride alone." I leaned over and spat onto the ground. This seemed like something Charlie McCoy would do, so I did it.

"Maybe you don't think so now, but just you wait until the ruling class brings their hammer down and crushes you like a bug. Then even cowboys will need a union." The anarcho-syndicalist glanced right and left, then up at the sky and then down at the ground. "Everything will change one day. You'll see. The working class won't be compliant forever. It's going to rise up. That's not an issue. The only issue is when. Then justice will come. Justice will come for everybody and everything will be redeemed."

I could tell that the young man was starting to get excited. The veins on his neck were like in bold relief and he was starting to gesture a lot, like he couldn't contain himself in his body but needed to jump out of himself. I wanted to get out of the conversation but I wanted to do it without upsetting him any more than he already was. "Well, look," me and Charlie McCoy said, "I gotta go."

"You don't like me, do you?" he asked. That hint of tears was coming back to him. Me and Charlie felt awfully sorry for this guy, what with his tattered jeans and his wild hair and the deep stink all around and about him and his anarcho-syndicalism with its attempt to do something that could never be done. "No, no, I like you. I just gotta get going." I smiled, trying to buck the kid up. "You know the buttes and the range and everything."

"That's all right. You don't have to come up with any excuses. I get it." The kid stood up and started to move away. "Anyway, I know I stink."

"That ain't it," I said, Charlie McCoy rising up off the bench and putting his hand on the kid's shoulder. "I just got a lot to do and not much time to do it in."

The kid swiveled on me with a swift and strange sense of fury. "What? Gotta mow the back forty? Gotta round up some strays? Gotta join a posse and hunt down some outlaws?" The words were hissing out of the young man's teeth, his eyes had gone narrow and his cheeks were red. "You're just like everybody else, cowboy: absolutely totally one hundred percent full of bullshit." He swiveled back around, tossing a sardonic, "Have a nice day," over his shoulder as he left.

I decided not to pursue him. There wasn't anything to gain by it. Not when his mind was so clearly made up, locked and sealed and delivered. At least he had my five dollars. Maybe that would make a difference later. Charlie McCoy liked to help people, especially drifters. Charlie McCoy had a soft spot for them. Sure, Charlie could be tough when he had to: nobody ever made the mistake of underestimating the raw toughness of Charlie McCoy. But that toughness could melt, and real quickly too, if a damsel in distress suddenly made an appearance or a fellow cowpoke needed a hand, or an anarcho-syndicalist did.

On the bus ride home, Charlie and I felt real good about the excursion. Sure, the encounter with the little Mexican kid had been a little spooky and the exchange with the Wobbly a little weird, but at least no one was dead.

14

The excursion with Charlie McCoy had gone so well that I regained my confidence and decided that I didn't need to lie low any longer. I could be who I wanted to be and trust that nothing would happen. Not everything had to end in murder. That much was obvious. The killing by Buddy Dickson was just due to Buddy's bad nature, as he was basically psychotic anyway, but he had been retired, so that was over and done with. And the killing by Glenda McPhee was a justifiable self-defense-type homicide—I mean what was she supposed to do anyway with that man about to cut her balls off? So there was that. Everyone else had been fine and so I could proceed with my adventures.

But what would be next? That question had me pondering for a few days as I considered the options. Maybe I should pretend to be an old cripple with a walker. But that wouldn't be much fun. Maybe an eccentric, like a tinkerer, an inventor, his garage full of winches and pulleys and pedals and beakers and manuals and everything. That could be interesting. Or maybe I should be a private detective. That sounded good. I'd always wanted to be a detective, sort of like Columbo with the cigars and the trench coat and all that. I sifted through a lot of possibilities, considering them from all kinds of angles, until I finally decided on something and got all the clothes I needed from the Internet and tried everything out in front of the mirror, the voice and the clothes and the stance and the gait and everything, and then I went out and put it on display in public.

It was funny. No one even shot a second glance at me. It was almost like I wasn't even there. In fact, it reminded me of all those years at the DMV. Anonymous, a nonentity, everyone looking through me, not at me.

But this was a good sign, as I didn't want anyone staring at me. I just wanted the character to blend in, to fit, to be one with the crowd. Yet who would imagine that Tom Small, inventor, would blend in so well, what with his thick eye-glasses and his Dodgers baseball cap slung low on his head, almost covering his ears, and the clip-on pocket protector he had inserted into his shirt, and the creased white slacks and the white socks and the loafers? Plus, I tried to fit Tom Small with an almost permanent-type smile, as it seemed like he was the kind of person who was always cheery and bright, his mind continually working on new possibilities, new innovations, new inventions. I decided to send Tom Small to the Natural History Museum, as this seemed like the perfect spot to be. So Tom Small took the 207 bus to Exposition and then transferred to the Expo line and took it one stop to the museum.

It was a lovely day and Tom Small and I decided to stroll through the rose garden before hitting the Natural History Museum. There were a couple of wedding parties out in the garden and they were having their pictures taken. They were all Hispanics and dressed up real crisply and nice and formal, bright colors, whites and mauves and reds. Everyone seemed so happy and so was I. I was Tom Small, inventor, and I had plenty of pens and pencils in my pocket and lots of things to cook up and imagine, projects to wrap up and patents waiting in line to be verified and confirmed. It was an exciting life, being an inventor. Wherever you looked, things could be improved. Innovation was there to be had, it only had to be innovated. Which maybe sounds silly and even stupid, but it's true. Take the airplane, for instance. How'd the Wright Brothers come up with their ideas? Did you know that the idea for the curvature of airplane wings came from one of the Wright Brothers gazing at a piece of cardboard and noticing how it kind of could fold and bend into various shapes? So the innovation was right there, lying there, waiting, until it was innovated, see. That's how science works.

Like right here in the Rose Garden. Yes, like maybe there's an innovation waiting right here, suspended in a sort of mid-air condition of nothingness until the right person comes along and snatches it out of the air. And then they tinker with it, draw up some sketches and diagrams, write up a description and do all the other stuff that needs to be done, and then file a patent with the U.S. Patent Office and who knows, maybe get rich.

Tom Small and I knew all about this stuff. Tom Small was on the verge of a major breakthrough in aeronautics. But it was something he couldn't talk about, not even with his best friend or his wife, that is, if he'd had a best friend or a wife. Because he was too preoccupied with his work to indulge in those kinds of things. Those kinds of things were for normal people and if there was anything Tom Small was not, it was normal. Tom Small was unusually bright, unusually ambitious, unusually gifted. He had been precocious ever since he was a child in Joplin, Missouri. His father was the manager of a hardware store and his mother taught science at the local high school. This made for a perfect background for an inveterate tinkerer and soon-to-be inventor. Tom Small built his own sewing machine out of wayward stuff that was just lying around the house. He did this when he was eleven years old. That was the kind of person Tom Small was.

I liked Tom Small. I felt good in his body and he felt good in mine. There was something incredibly happy about him, an attitude forever positive and leaning towards everything that was gentle and pure and good. Tom Small was about as far away as you could get from Buddy Dickson. If Buddy Dickson was all bad, Tom Small was all good. Tom Small had his ideas and that's all he needed. Well, that and drafting paper and pencils and a pocket calculator and all that. If Buddy Dickson saw every situation as a situation in which he could find some sort of carnal satisfaction, Tom Small saw every situation as a situation in which he could find some sort of intellectual satisfaction. For Buddy Dickson, everything was destruction and self-satisfaction. For Tom Small, everything was creation and self-realization.

Not that Tom Small was a saint. He had his faults. But in a way they were positive faults, if there is such a thing. For instance, he couldn't stand bullies and he was intolerant of anyone with bad manners, like young guys that didn't give up their seats in the bus to old people. He hated that and he had to hold himself back whenever he saw anything like that happen. 'Cause he was afraid that if he intervened something even worse might happen.

Me and Tom Small decided we'd had enough of Mexican wedding pictures and rows of roses and so we went into the Natural History Museum. All the dioramas there sparked Tom Small's imagination. Instead of separate displays of the saber-tooth tigers and the wooly mammoths and all the rest of them, Tom Small envisioned one combined display that could be joined together on pneumatic wheels and could roll through one another so that all the animals would pass through each other's terrain. Tom Small also imagined a pedestrian walkway which would go down deep underneath the displays and reveal the sub-surface of the soil as well as the geologic features. This walkway would also go above the displays and show the birds and the different levels of the atmosphere and the chemical composition of the strata of the air.

Tom Small and I sat on a bench and I took out his notebook and sketched out a design for these innovations, making a note to myself and Tom Small to send an email to the director of the Natural History Museum about these plans. Then Tom Small felt a pang and realized that he and I hadn't eaten anything all day long so he went into the café and ordered fish tacos and a lemonade. While Tom Small and I ate our meal we took note of all the families of diverse ethnicities and backgrounds that were visiting the museum and eating at the café. This really heartened Tom Small, as to him it signified a future in which all these young children would grow up to be naturalists or chemists or inventors or at least tinkerers, people who were willing to do DIY without having to cough up money for a handyman. And the starting point for this future chock-full of scientists and engineers was right here in the Museum of Natural History. This place was like the womb of a tomorrow that would revolutionize the planet in cascades of innovations.

Sipping on his lemonade, Tom Small was very happy. So happy that he took out his notebook again and started to sketch out a blueprint for the future, a blueprint that would incorporate innovation into every waking moment of the night and day. Of course it was only a vague outline of a plan right now, but Tom Small and I were certain that it could be filled in bit by bit, one little bit at a time. Then Tom Small felt the urge to pee rising up in him, and I felt it too, so Tom Small and I went into the bathroom and locked ourselves in a stall. Tom Small and I thought we might have to poop too, so we sat down on the toilet and waited for something to happen.

Tom Small and I were right: it was a poop as well as a pee and we were happy we had sat down on the toilet instead of getting all mixed up and first taking a pee standing up before we had to sit down to take the poop. We unlatched the door, stepped out of the stall and started to wash our hands. Tom Small looked at the mirror and I noticed that Tom Small's pocket protector was set a little awry so I straightened it back into place.

I felt the man's hand before I heard his voice. His hand clamped down on my wrist as I stood there at the sink and then he said, "What the fuck do you think you're doing here?" I looked over and saw the man. He was a big white guy, a biker, with one of those cut-off jean jackets that they wear, all sloppy and dirty and looking like it was smeared with puke and snot and stuff, and a t-shirt with a picture of Jim Morrison on it and filthy blue jeans that looked like they had deliberately been smeared with grease and oil and gunk. He was grinning and he had a full beard so long it hung halfway down to his belly button. He turned just a little and I got a glimpse of the back of his jacket. It read Sons of Satan, San Bernardino.

"What's the problem?" Tom Small asked.

For some reason this question made the biker grin. "Oh, I think you know what the problem is. Matter of fact, I think you got a real clear idea of the problem." He was still holding onto my wrist, clamping down even harder, I'd say, judging from the level of pain Tom Small and I were starting to feel.

"Actually I don't," Tom Small and I said, our voices falling in together.

"You think you can get away with it," the biker said, dropping the grin and getting real serious, a sense of menace in his voice, like something very bad had happened and he had been sent to straighten it out. Was this guy a cop? One of those undercover detectives you always see in television shows? But if that was so, why was he lying in wait for me? Did he know about Buddy Dickson and Glenda McPhee? Were the cops closing in on me? What the hell was going on?

"Get away with what?" I tried to say this with total innocence, as if I knew nothing about nothing and that was it.

"Sneaking into the bathroom, huh? Lying here in wait, huh?"

The biker drew in real close to me so his face was right up against mine. I could smell his breath stinking of what seemed like a weird mixture of garlic and beer and rum and I could see beads of sweat forming on his forehead.

"Lying here in wait for what?" Tom Small and I asked, trying to keep that totally innocent tone going, which was pretty easy to do, given the fact that Tom Small had never done anything wrong.

"Lying here in wait for some little kid to come along, aren't you, you sick fuck." Now he was holding me and Tom Small with one hand and wagging his index finger at us with the other.

"I'm not doing anything," Tom Small said. "I'm just urinating and defecating."

That got the biker laughing. "Oh sure, all you're doing is taking a pee and a poop." Then he grabbed Tom Small by his shirt and rammed him hard against the mirror, so hard the mirror cracked and pieces of glass fell to the floor and a bright spot of blood exploded on the back of Tom Small's head.

We quickly did a check and Tom Small and I weren't hurt too badly: we just crumpled up a little bit after getting our heads rammed against the mirror and so we were now bent forward, catching our breath while our blood dripped onto the floor. But then we sprung back and gazed into the deep brown eyes of the biker. "You're making a mistake here," we said, trying to get the biker to stop what he was doing before it was too late.

Then the biker made a bad move. "I'm making a mistake? I'm making a mistake!" He slung his fist back as if getting it ready to send it right into Tom Small's nose. "Why, you lousy little shitty pervert!"

Then he swung the fist forward towards my face, which was also Tom Small's face, but he only made it halfway there as Tom Small had ripped a pen out of his pocket and had plunged it deep into the biker's right eye.

For what seemed like a long moment everything was

suspended. It was like the pen stuck into the eye had pinned everything into a frozen tableau, Tom Small and I staring at the pen stuck into the biker's eye and the biker staring at me and Tom Small. It was like the biker was trying to figure out what had happened with this pen sticking out of his eye. Everything had been going in one direction and now it was going in another. Everything had been in motion and now it was still. It was so still and so silent, Tom Small and I could hear the distant voices of families out in the corridor and the humming of pipes, and somewhere far off the clattering of dishes in the café.

Then the biker fell forward onto his hands and knees. He said one word, 'Fuck,' and then he crumpled down flat and then he took a few more breaths and then he appeared to be dead. Tom Small and I kneeled next to the man and felt for a pulse and listened for a breath, but there was nothing. The biker was indeed dead.

Tom Small and me leaned back on our haunches and tried to figure out what to do. We couldn't stay there, that was for sure. And it also didn't seem too smart to just leave the body, but what else could we do?

Just at that moment a boy came into the bathroom, sandy-haired, lean, maybe ten years old. "What's wrong with him?" asked the kid, indicating the biker laying splayed out on the floor.

"I think he's sick," said Tom Small. "He threw up something awful."

"Oh," was all the kid said and then he stepped up to a urinal and took a piss. Tom Small and I just stayed there in place, frozen, waiting for the kid to leave. It was rather awkward, to say the least, what with the body of the biker on the floor and the blood starting to spread out from his head and the kid taking a pee and me and Tom Small just standing there, trying to act like everything was completely natural. As soon as the kid left,

15

Well, that was weird. What went wrong? Or did anything go wrong? Tom Small had seemed so harmless, so totally concentrated on inventions and innovations, without a bad bone in his body. I thought I was safe with him. I thought everyone was safe with him. But then something had happened. The Son of Satan had appeared and he had asked for it, right? What else were Tom and I supposed to do? Maybe it would've been better if Tom had found a solution to the situation that wasn't so drastic. Maybe he should have just bolted out the door and then run as fast as he could. But the biker with his great big body had blocked any chance of escape. So Tom Small had taken one of his trusty pens out of his pocket protector and that had solved the problem. Sort of. Except that now there was a dead man in the bathroom of the Natural History Museum and right about now the homicide detectives would be interviewing the kid who had taken the pee and anybody else who may have noticed us.

But then that was all right, wasn't it? Because everyone would describe someone who looked like Tom Small and there was no Tom Small. He didn't exist except as my own creation and so Tom Small and I were safe. Right?

The Expo line and then the transfer to the bus ride home all took forever, each piece of track and every inch of the road elongated and monstrous. I had taken the precaution of taking off Tom Small's glasses and his pocket protector and tossing them into a trashcan. But even so, I kept expecting a police helicopter to come swooping overhead, looming suspended in place, rotors beating the air, and then some squad cars coming down upon us, sirens wailing. But nothing happened and no one seemed to notice us. I was still anonymous, unknown, a cipher, and that was my safety and my security.

Or so I thought.

But then I had to wonder: had I tried to have this confrontation with the biker? Was I looking for an opportunity to kill? I had to admit, when Tom Small and I plunged that pen into the biker's eye, it felt good. Exciting. Very exciting. As if I had touched upon the very essence of life. As if by taking life, I was receiving life. But it wasn't just me and Tom Small who were receiving life. It was also the biker. That pen plunging into his eye had been the most transcendent moment of that guy's life. For in that moment everything in his life slammed together into one bright point and then everything disintegrated into blazing oblivion. That moment was miraculous. It couldn't be beat. So it wasn't only for me and Tom Small, not by a mile. It was for the biker as well. As a matter of fact, more for him than for us. As he was really the only one who truly experienced that moment right down to its nub. The rest of us were just spectators. Even though we were the ones who had driven the pen into the man's skull.

When I got home, I slumped down onto the sofa and just lay there for what seemed like hours. I thought about giving up the whole enterprise. After all, three people were dead. Not only were they dead, but they had been murdered, murdered by me and Buddy Dickson, murdered by me and Glenda McPhee, and murdered by me and Tom Small, so that it was pretty easy to see that the common denominator was me. Well, and murder. Me and murder. So I couldn't blame this on Buddy and Glenda and Tom and their psychotic personalities or their predilection for being in the wrong place at the wrong time or their over-developed sense of self-protection. I couldn't just pretend that I was some kind of unwitting accomplice, an innocent bystander to their violence. No, I had been there. I had participated and, if anything, they were the unwitting accomplices and the innocent bystanders. I was the killer. I was the one with the blood on his hands. It was me. It was Lloyd Stollman. He was the murderer and he was me.

But so what?

And what I mean by that is that I didn't care. No, that's not right. I cared all right. I cared a lot. But I cared in the other direction. And what I mean by that is that I liked doing it. Liked doing it? I loved doing it. There was just something about it, that moment of death, witnessing it like that, that thrilled me beyond belief. I mean I'm sorry, you probably think I'm a monster or a creep or something, but I'm just trying to be honest here and that's what I felt and that's what I still feel. Even now. With the police closing in and all options over.

But I'm getting ahead of my story. Let me just stick with what happened and how it happened, one thing after another.

So I sat slumped on the couch, still in Tom Small's costume, though I'd discarded his glasses. I supposed it would have been best to lie low for a week or two but that kind of caution had left me. I just didn't care anymore. Or I did care but not enough to stop me from doing what I was doing, and doing it when and where and how I wanted to do it. It was like I was on some sort of carnival ride and couldn't get off. Things were set in a certain way and that's the way they were and there was nothing anyone could do to change course. I could only make decisions about what particular steps to take next, like what character I wanted to be and things like that. I couldn't make decisions about the overall nature of what I was doing: that had already been decided.

But that sounds like someone or some thing had made the decision for me. And maybe that's exactly what I meant. Maybe there was something bigger than me that was organizing this whole thing, driving it, putting it into place. And all I was doing was going along with the plan, a plan that I couldn't stop, a plan I couldn't resist, because it was my life and my life had been laid out like this with Buddy Dickson and Glenda McPhee and Tom Small and everything they had done with me.

But that didn't make sense. 'Cause if it did, it would mean that the devil or some strange God-like thing or nature itself or the fate of the universe or something was guiding this whole thing along. Well, not only guiding it, but actually doing it. As if I, with all my disguises, Charlie McCoy and Tom Small and everyone else, was completely lined up with this thing and was just doing its bidding, like we were puppets.

And that would also mean that I had no responsibility for anything that had happened. And wouldn't that be convenient? Guilt-free, scot-free, nothing sticking to me, Teflon-like, because instead of me and Buddy and Charlie and Tom and Glenda doing all this stuff on our own, we had done it with God or the devil or Fate or whatever, and so we were just cogs, just little pinwheels, and had nothing to do with anything that had happened. God had meant for that Son of Satan to die in the bathroom of the Natural History Museum with a pen in his eye, inserted by Tom Small. The devil had ordered that the black guy who wanted to have sex with Glenda should be strangled, his life seeping out underneath the freeway. Fate had demanded that Buddy Dickson plunge a knife into the guts of that innocent waitress, Rita White. None of that makes sense except in a universe gone haywire, and I still believed that the world made sense. At least I believed that then, despite everything that had happened.

It was all so confusing that it made my head ache. And that's when I decided I should take Charlie McCoy out for a Thai massage.

16

And yet I ended up dressing like Glenda McPhee. I didn't even think twice about it. It wasn't like I decided anything. It just happened. But as I slipped on the panties and strapped on the bra (that behind-the-back motion to clip the bra together really a hard one for a sixty-two-year-old man) and then pulled on the dress and the last thing, the high heels, I knew why I was putting on Glenda McPhee.

I liked being a woman. The panties felt so good against my cock. Even the bra with the falsies felt comfortable, as if I should have been wearing them all along, and it was a shame I had discovered them so late in life. Sure, the high heels were a challenge, my ankles a little wobbly, my calves all achy after walking half a block, but yet and still, being a woman was a welcome change. It was nice being the object of attention instead of the person who was always supposed to pay attention. Plus, once I got on the bus, I could very gently rub my thighs together and that would cause my panties to rub up against my dick and get a pretty good erection going.

Even though I was Glenda instead of Charlie, I was still heading to the Thai massage parlor I frequented, the one up on Hollywood Boulevard near Serrano. Touch of Asia, it's called, and I was a regular. I was always with Ting. Ting was so nice to me. Always gave me a thorough full-body massage before finishing me off, as they say. I always gave her a good tip, even a hundred-dollar bill at Christmas and Valentine's Day, or sometimes just because I felt like it. Ting had beautiful lips and these small tits that were so perfect, nice and rounded and just right. She let me suck on them once. For my birthday. My sixtieth. What a treat that was. And Ting had one of those nice small pert Asian asses. Wow. I was so lucky I had found her.

So I wanted to walk in there as Glenda McPhee and see if Ting recognized me. I was betting that she wouldn't. But I could have been wrong. Ting's no dummy and she's seen a lot of people come through the doors of the Touch of Asia. She must have seen all types in all shapes and sizes. She's kind of a sociologist in a way, or would it be an anthropologist? Whatever, she certainly is a psychologist, as she has to figure out people and their sexual habits and proclivities in a millionth of a millisecond or so.

On the bus ride up to Hollywood Boulevard I sat down near the front with no one next to me and then I remembered why me and Glenda had wanted to get into her clothes again. It was for the bus ride. The way the throb of the engine rumbled against Glenda's panties and sent Glenda's vagina shivering, the tingle of it all going right up my spine. Almost immediately I got an erection, a really big one too.

There's nothing like having a boner when you're dressed as a woman. Me and Glenda loved it. It was her and me and the panties and the bus and the boner, all of us together, having a thrill.

Luckily I had my big black purse to cover my lap, otherwise the erection would have been sticking straight up and I would have been arrested or something. At Olympic, a wizened old Korean lady got on the bus and sat next to me. She was wearing a tinted visor and she was carrying an empty shopping bag. She looked at me and smiled, and me and Glenda smiled back. My erection deflated for a moment as the presence of this lady distracted me and Glenda from the feeling of my dick against Glenda's lacy panties. But then I turned to the window and shut out the Korean lady and my erection bounced right back, roaring into action. I was kind of afraid I might have an orgasm right there in the bus. I wanted to save that for Ting, of course. And, being that I'm an older man now, sixty-two with sixty-three looming ahead in just a few months, I can't get it up over and over again like I used to when I was a youngster and had to walk between classes at high school with a binder kind of angled over my groin to hide the boner I was always nursing along.

Anyway, there was nothing to worry about, as my erection just stood there, suspended kind of like, not deflating into flaccidity but not leaping into climax either. I was a good boy and so was Glenda. Well, I mean she was a good *girl,* right? For she was the girl and I was the boy and we were out together, almost like we were on a date or something.

Once we got to Hollywood Boulevard, I got off of the bus and Glenda did too, and we walked the couple of blocks to the Touch of Asia. Boy, those high heels were awful. I almost tumbled over into the street, that's how shaky I was. But Glenda could handle it a little better than I could, of course, and so we made it to the front door of the massage parlor intact and then we entered, me and Glenda together. What a pair, the real odd couple, I'd say.

The reception area in the Touch of Asia is dimly lit, candles glowing everywhere, and after the brightness of the day outside, it took a moment until Glenda and I could see anything. Ah, but yes, there was Mrs. Lee and she smiled at me, but I couldn't tell if she was smiling at Glenda or smiling at me being Glenda or both or neither. I mean, had she recognized me behind the outfit?

"How can I help you?" Mrs. Lee asked in that sweet voice of hers, the voice that makes you feel like there's nothing weird or perverted or strange about showing up at a massage parlor in the middle of the day in a dress, and then I also knew that the disguise had worked because if she thought it was just me, just

Lloyd Stollman, a regular who had been there dozens and dozens of times, she would have called me by name and then asked how everything was and so on. But she didn't do any of that, and so I knew she didn't know who the heck I was. That is, unless she was just being polite until I revealed who I was, Glenda and Lloyd, one and together, separate and united. And it wasn't so weird to have a woman come in there, if that's what you're thinking, as I had seen plenty of women in there before. A woman needs a massage just like a guy does, and maybe they were getting their own "finishing off" bits as well, I don't know, and it's not my business to know that anyway, is it? I don't think so.

I told Mrs. Lee that I had heard that a woman named Ting gave the best massages at the Touch of Asia and then she told me that Ting was with a customer, but that if I didn't mind waiting for ten minutes, Ting could see me. Of course I didn't mind, I told her, and so me and Glenda sat down and I picked up a *People Magazine* and started leafing through it. I love *People Magazine*. You can learn all sorts of stuff in there. Like who's had a baby and who's dating who, you know, all the stuff about the stars and everything, and then they have stuff about regular people too, people who have overcome tremendous odds, like schizophrenics who get advanced degrees or people who cannot walk but manage to swim the English Channel, stuff like that. Sitting there in the reception area of the Touch of Asia on Hollywood Boulevard, me with Glenda and Glenda with me, I wondered if *People Magazine* would do a story on us. We'd have to leave out some stuff, of course, like the black guy lying there dead underneath the Santa Monica Freeway, but other than that, it could make an interesting human interest story. DMV employee for twenty-five years transforms into woman in high heels. Okay, maybe it's too weird for most people, but it is interesting, nevertheless, surely that can't be denied. And of course, with the gorgeous way Glenda looked and her makeup and her big tall stature and everything, the photographs would be terrific. But I quickly discarded the notion, as too much attention might not be the best thing right at the moment. Stay low, kind of underground, that's the ticket.

Finally, Ting stepped into the lobby, looking just as beautiful as always. She looked at me and smiled. "Are you Glenda?" she asked. She was so beautiful. I practically came in my panties right then and there. I answered that I was Glenda all right, and then she smiled even more and led me back to her room, a room which I knew very well of course. There were the blown-up photos of downtown Seoul on the walls and a carved wooden Buddha in the corner and then a big picture of Lebron James, as Ting is a big Lakers fan and a devotee of Lebron.

"Change and lie down and I'll be back in a minute."

I wasn't sure that I could wait that long because by then my boner was practically bursting out of Glenda's panties. Besides, I wanted Ting to be present when I took off my clothes and presented myself as Lloyd Stollman, regular.

"Do you have to go?" I asked, trying to put a girlish sort of plaintive wail into my voice.

"Well, no, I can stay," said Ting, always eager to please the customer. "If that's what you want."

"That's what I want," I said, and I started by kicking off those brutal shoes and then pulling down my skirt. My blouse covered my panties so my erection wasn't visible yet. I took a moment and gazed at Ting with what I hoped was a sexy smile. "Are you ready for this, Ting?" I asked.

"Oh, I'm ready, Glenda," said Ting.

Then I pulled down my panties and they kind of slapped over my boner and then my boner popped up straight, sticking out from the bottom section of my blouse, right below the last button.

Ting shrieked involuntarily and actually hopped, putting her hand over her mouth to clam the yelp that wanted to come out of her. She pointed at my boner, sticking up there in the air. "What is that?" she asked.

"That's my penis. I'm a man." I whipped the wig off and shook out my hair. "It's Lloyd, Lloyd Stollman."

I was smiling real big, proud of both the straightness of my erection sticking up out of my disguise and also of the fact that my disguise had worked so well.

But then Ting's yelp turned into laughter, a bellyful roaring up out of her. "Lloyd, what are you doing in that dress?"

She was pointing at me and she was laughing and I started to get the feeling that I had made a terrible mistake.

I gestured vaguely to the dress and then to my body. "I don't know," I said, "I thought it would be fun. I thought you would like it."

"Oh Lloyd." She was still laughing and I wanted that to stop. She was still pointing at me and I wanted that to stop too. "I thought there was something weird about Glenda."

Okay, so now I was getting angry, really angry. "There's nothing weird about Glenda McPhee. She's a very sweet lady, in fact."

"Oh, I'm sure."

Ting had stopped laughing, but she was still smiling. And it was kind of a creepy smile too. Like she couldn't wait to tell Mrs. Lee and the other girls all about this bizarre customer she had, Lloyd Stollman, who had come to a session dressed up as a woman. I had always thought Ting was so nice, but now I was having to think about that assessment. Maybe she was just like the other women, a bitch just waiting for the opportunity to laugh at a guy. Even one standing in the middle of the room with a big boner that was deflating, and fast. Or maybe especially at a guy standing in the middle of the room with a big boner fast deflating. Women! All alike, heartless and cruel.

"At least Glenda isn't working at a massage parlor on Hollywood Boulevard."

"Oh Lloyd, there's no need to get mean."

She stepped towards me and made a vague gesture, which seemed to indicate that she was trying to restart the session, clear the air and kind of regain a sense of everything being ordinary, or as ordinary as a massage parlor on Hollywood Boulevard can be.

"You want the usual?" Her smile went sort of seductive as she asked: "Or maybe something special? No extra charge?"

"I don't know…" My voice was real quiet, I was almost whispering, barely audible. "Maybe I should just go…"

"Don't do that, Lloyd."

She reached out and touched my penis. Stroked it, and it began to revive a little. "Don't you want to stay and have some fun."

There was nothing I could do. She had me. Women. What power they have! I had wanted to run out of there, but now here I was, lying down on the massage table and getting a full-body job, with free extras as a finishing-off treat. Well, Glenda McPhee was having a pretty interesting day, that much had to be said.

After it was over, me and Glenda put myself back together again. I glanced in the mirror just to get the wig on straight, and I saw Ting looking at me as I was looking at Glenda. Ting, realizing that she had been caught, smiled and said with what seemed like total sincerity: "You look good, Glenda. You look real good."

I couldn't help it: I blushed. And then I smiled. "Thanks, Ting," I said. "That means a lot. Coming from you."

"You fooled me, right?"

"Right." A sense of pride surged through me. I had fooled her. And Mrs. Lee. And that was really something, considering that they saw all kinds of types in all kinds of shapes and sizes coming into the Touch of Asia. Glenda and me were a great team. We had something going, the two of us. Something special. Something real special. "We fooled you, me and Glenda." I slipped into my high heels and then took my wallet out of my purse.

"No money today," Ting said, reaching out and closing my wallet and setting it gently into my purse.

"What?" I said. I wasn't quite sure I had heard that right, and if I had heard it right, if I had really comprehended what she had said.

"It's on the house. From me to you." Ting clasped my purse shut and then kissed me full on the lips. "You've been such a great friend. You deserve it."

That was so nice. She hadn't said client or customer or john or any of the other words used to describe men in my position; she had said, "friend." Wow. That was so nice. I insisted on giving her a twenty and then I made my way to the street, nodding to Mrs. Lee as I did so.

Out on the sidewalk, I felt grand. Real grand. Everything had gone according to plan, or even better than the plan. Me and Glenda had fooled Ting and Mrs. Lee and then I had gotten a freebie from Ting. What more could a guy and a girl ask for?

It was at that moment, walking down the sidewalk to the bus stop at the intersection at Hollywood and Western, that I finally realized what I was doing. I was thinking of myself as a man and as a woman, as a man and a woman combined, as a girl and a boy melded together. And here's the other thing I realized, and this really surprised me: It felt right. it felt natural. But not only that, it felt like it was more natural and more right than thinking of myself as merely a man or as merely a woman. Lloyd Stollman by himself or Glenda McPhee by herself were not complete beings, but Lloyd Stollman and Glenda McPhee as one combined being was a total and complete package, psychologically sound and physically hearty. The combination of the two was so much better than the singularity of the one. And it seemed to me that all human beings should be made like this, half female and half male, interchangeable parts, with one taking over while the other rests, and so on and so forth, trading places like that. I was convinced that it would lead to a much healthier world, with men and women developing a deeper understanding of one another because they would actually be one and the other. Doesn't that make sense?

So, my physical being all perky due to Ting's attentions, and my mental state all popping due to these thoughts I was having, I boarded the bus to go back home. I thought my newfound condition of mental hygiene would just continue on as it was, perky and popping, but by the time we crossed Fountain, I was starting to feel real blue. It's so sad, happiness vanishes so quickly. And most of the time there doesn't seem like there's any reason for it to disappear, it just goes, vanishing without a shred of logic. But maybe there was some rationale to its disappearance, at least in this case. I wasn't a man and a woman. I wasn't male and female combined into some sort of divine union. I was just Lloyd Stollman, a solitary guy who was dressing up in different outfits. Charlie McCoy, Tom Small, Benny Monger, Buddy Dickson, Glenda McPhee. These characters or masks or roles or people were not real. They were just figments. They were just pretend people dressed up in costumes.

And yet they were real too. Maybe too real. All but two of them had killed somebody. Only Benny and Charlie had managed to escape that fate. Only the cowboy and the queer were innocent. Only the cowboy and the queer were safe and secure. But were the rest of them really guilty? Maybe Buddy was guilty too. I could accept that, but Glenda and Tom they had just kind of stumbled into murder. It wasn't their fault. Wrong place, wrong time. Right?

Then suddenly it occurred to me, and what a dummy and an idiot I was not to think of this earlier: I shouldn't be out with Glenda. She might get caught and then where would I be? In jail with her and that's not where I belonged. But how could Glenda get caught? Yes, of course, she had strangled that black man underneath the Santa Monica Freeway, and I had been there with her when she had done that, but no one could tie her to that crime as no one had seen it happen. Not in that lonely wedge of dirt underneath the roaring traffic overhead and not one of the drivers swiftly moving above being even aware of what was happening beneath them, the white hands on the black throat and the life seeping out of the man. So it was all right for me to be out with Glenda because no one suspected her and anyway, she wasn't the same person as me. She was Glenda and I was me, and yes, we did things together, but there was quite a bit of difference between us, as anyone with half a brain could see. So everything was all right. Great, in fact. Look at how things had gone with Ting. She hadn't even recognized me and then when she did, she gave me a freebie with the works.

And now here I was back in the bus and my dick was heading into a semi again as it rubbed against those lacey panties I was wearing. Geez, sixty-two years old and I can't keep this thing down, at least when I'm dressed up as Glenda McPhee and I'm wearing high heels and ladies underwear.

17

I needed something new. So Clarence Finnegan came into view. He wore a bow tie and, boy, tying that thing took a while to figure out. And he wore a seersucker suit, saddle shoes and black-rimmed glasses. Thank god for my government pension, cause outfitting all these people wasn't cheap, especially if you wanted to do it right, which of course I did.

Clarence was independently wealthy, one of the eccentric rich, I guess you could call him. His grandfather had invented the forklift and his father had been an international playboy and had hung out with the Kennedy brothers when JFK and RFK were taking turns with Marilyn Monroe at the Ambassador Hotel. Clarence had rebelled against his father's loose ways and had been a teetotaler his whole life, as well as a virgin until the age of twenty-four. He served on the boards of various charities and dabbled in watercolors. He had been married once to a Filipina, but there were no children and his ex-wife had returned to Manila.

Given his inclinations about art, I decided I should take Clarence to the Los Angeles County Museum of Art on our first excursion. Clarence really liked all the antiquities there, even the Olmec stuff which I personally find a little too weird. But Clarence is much more sophisticated about such things than I am. After all, the only art I have ever been exposed to were the millions of headshots I had taken at the DMV, and that hardly qualifies. Just one face after another, filing through in a big blur. But Clarence could look at one painting for like fifteen minutes and see all sorts of different stuff in it. For instance, for the first little while, he might be just getting like a general impression of the thing, its subject matter of course, and then the composition and the basic color scheme and all that. But then he'd really start scrutinizing it until I didn't even know what the heck he was looking at, but pretty soon he'd come up with something. Like how some random-looking red patch in a far corner of the canvas matched the red cheeks of a maid in another corner. Or how the angle of a swing was set against the backdrop of the skyscrapers behind it. Really detailed stuff that I had never noticed before. And that was one of the great things about being with these people: how they taught me about all sorts of stuff I had never even considered. Even Buddy Dickson had taught me some stuff, like how neat it feels to be dressed up so sharp and what it feels like to say whatever the hell is on our mind, regardless of the consequences. And Charlie McCoy, he had taught me about the love of roaming and roving on a wide-open plain, even if that wide-open plain were the streets of downtown L.A. And of course Glenda McPhee had given me insights into the mind of a female and she'd also taught me how it feels to have a cock growing strong against the cool fabric of a woman's panties. And now here was Clarence Finnegan, giving me a lesson in art appreciation. Yes, I was finally getting the education I deserved, a well-rounded education from all different perspectives.

After about two hours of gazing at art, Clarence and I needed a break so we went out into the plaza and watched people as we sipped a coffee. It was a Saturday and families were out, getting some art into their systems. The kids seemed happy to be there, like they knew it was special and so they were special too. And the parents seemed all taken with themselves, as if it was a good deed to take their children to an art establishment and like it made them enlightened or something. Maybe I sound a little cynical about it, but hardly anything is ever done on this planet just for itself. There's always secondary motivations, or things that seem like secondary motivations that are really primary motivations. Like a guy's not nice to a girl just because he's nice. He's looking for something else, right? And I'm not talking just about sex, though of course that's one of the things that might be involved. He wants to be seen as cool or gallant or masculine or something. And maybe underneath all that, he's yearning for sex and maybe even love, who knows. Or a person like Clarence doesn't give to a charity just to give to a charity. He wants to be seen as an esteemed member of the community and all that. And Clarence understands that. I mean, at least that's what he told me. If you want pure motivations, you need to look to the animals, not to human beings. That's my opinion. And it's Clarence's opinion as well. Funny how reality and fiction can get all jumbled together.

On the way home, Clarence and I almost got into some real trouble. The bus was pretty full, we were standing together in the aisle, and a bunch of young guys were sitting in the seats up next to the bus driver, the ones reserved for the handicapped and the elderly. So this old lady gets in and she has some shopping bags in her arms, and these guys don't move an inch. They don't even seem to notice her. They just keep listening to their I-Pads or their I-Phones or whatever the heck they are. Now, me, I don't care that much about this. I'm not going to interfere, as it's none of my business, and anyway, one of these young guys might bust me in the jaw if I go and intervene. But Clarence, he's not like that. He sees it as his civic duty and his moral obligation to interfere in such cases. Which to me is idiotic, not only because you might get busted in the jaw, but also because one lone person can't turn the tide in terms of righting wrongs and undoing evil and nabbing the bad guys and all that stuff. But, like I said, Clarence has a different view on this, so before I knew it, he was standing up in the middle of the aisle and bawling these young guys out for not giving up their seats.

"You moral degenerates," he cried. "Stand up this instant and allow this lady to sit down." And suddenly I was reminded of another old movie, *Beat the Devil*, and that very very English chap who plays the husband of Jennifer Jones, and that maybe, just maybe, I had gotten the inspiration for Clarence from that fellow, whatever the hell his name is.

I have to say that the young guys were really startled by this outburst, not just by the message but also by the messenger and the way in which the message was delivered. You could tell they were having trouble computing it all, and there I was in the middle of this tense silence, just hoping Clarence wouldn't shoot off his big stupid mouth anymore. Even the old lady Clarence was doing this for, even she looked kind of startled, and a little worried as well. She waved her hand in a slight gesture, indicating that she didn't need a seat that badly and that there was no need for Clarence to intervene, no matter how pure and noble his sentiments might be. She could see what was happening, just like I could, and she didn't want there to be any trouble because of her. But Clarence couldn't be deterred. It had become not only a matter of principle, but one of honor. And this honor thing that Clarence was all wrought up about, this was like something out of the nineteenth century, like in England or somewhere in Europe, and we were in Los Angeles in 2021. It was like Clarence had dropped into our midst from another time and another land and I couldn't do anything to straighten him out. He would just have to learn on his own. And so he actually said, "I am sorry, madam. But I must insist."

Then he turned to the boys and gave out his command again: "Arise, you louts, and relinquish a seat to this fine lady." Now I felt like we were going even further back in time, like to the days of Robin Hood and merry olde England and all that. It was so absurd that one of the "louts" started laughing and said, "Who the fuck are you, old man?"

That's when all hell broke loose. 'Cause Clarence wasn't about to stand for such backtalk, especially from what he considered a commoner, a piece of riff-raff, rabble.

"Arise, I said, or I shall conk you on the head!" This is actually what Clarence said, unbelievable as it sounds, bizarre as it was. I wished I could have made him stop, 'cause I was standing right there, of course, but he seemed to be operating on his own, way outside my control. Like he was an independent being, which is exactly what he was.

The kid laughed some more. "Go ahead and conk me all you want, old-timer," he said. It was hard to tell what this kid's background was. Maybe Latin but then maybe Persian or something. He was like maybe sixteen but he might have been as old as twenty-five. He was wearing loose baggy jeans and sandals, a Clippers t-shirt but a Lakers cap. "I wanna see this."

"Be my guest," Clarence said, and then before I could stop him, he leapt forward and tried to give a blow to the head of this kid. The lady whom Clarence was doing all this for shrieked and I did too. Clarence never got his blow in as the kid easily fended it off and then delivered a sock to Clarence's belly, which sent him straight down into the aisle, clutching his gut while I clutched mine as well.

The bus driver immediately pulled over and announced that he was calling the police. I was doing my best to get Clarence out of the aisle but he had been hit pretty hard and he could barely breathe, let alone stand. I could hear the kid laughing, and then he said "You asked for it, old man," and he moved to the door, pried it open and jumped off onto the curb and ran away.

I had to get Clarence out of there, not just for his sake or mine, but also because of what Buddy Dickson, Tom Small and

Glenda McPhee had gone and done. So I crawled to the back door, breathing hard, an ache in Clarence's belly where the kid had hit me, and then I pried open the door as well and rolled off the bus into the gutter. I could hear a siren in the distance so I knew I had to get out of there and fast. I staggered to my feet and made my way into the nearest establishment, which happened to be a Korean restaurant. I ran straight through the restaurant, with the customers gaping up at me from their plates of kimchi this and kimchi that. I headed straight for the back, hoping there was a rear entrance, and indeed there was, right past the kitchen and the restroom. Once out in back, I stopped running, as a guy in a bow tie and a seersucker suit is an easy enough target as it is, but a guy in a bow tie and a seersucker suit who is also running is a target made like super-ultra-visible. So I just tried to be calm, hoping the police would treat it as the minor incident and non-event that it was, and just shrug it off and continue on with more important duties without sending multiple squad cars and helicopters out after me and Clarence.

And indeed that's what must have happened, because glancing back I saw the bus moving through he intersection and the cop car heading in the opposite direction from the one in which I was headed, so the coast was clear and everything was cool. Clarence and I heaved a sigh of relief as an encounter with the police was just about the last thing I wanted and I gladly took Clarence Finnegan home and got him out of his duds.

Once I had become myself, I went to the fridge and popped open a beer. I tell you, there is nothing like a Bud after you have been out on the street, disguised as someone else. It's a real pause that refreshes. For being in a disguise is quite a tricky business, even when things go generally according to plan. 'Cause always at the edge of your consciousness is the possibility that everything might go wrong. There's a huge risk factor, as I guess is pretty obvious from this chronicle. But that risk factor is also what makes it so damn exciting. You feel like you're getting away with something, even if nothing out of the ordinary happens. And this was all new to me. I had been the type of person who never once in his life had tried to get away with anything at all. The straight and narrow had been my only mode of existence. I worked for the DMV for twenty-five years, for god's sake, what could be more straight and more narrow than that! But even in college and high school, I had never done anything even remotely wild or weird.

I guess the only things I had done that could be put in a column of wildness and weirdness (that is, prior to my present adventures) were my monthly treks to the Touch of Asia and Ting. But these had become so banal and routine that even they felt like they fit into the straight and the narrow. Well, okay, maybe the first few times I went to the massage parlor, sure, maybe those times, it felt risky and even a little dangerous. But I soon became a regular and so everything else about my visits there became regular as well.

But what I was doing now was incredibly risky and therefore incredibly thrilling. Every aspect of it was unbelievably adventurous as far as I was concerned, from the first glimmer of a new character flitting through my mind to the last moment of an expedition with that character out on the streets.

And yet there was something that was terribly wrong. And I'm not just referring to the dead people, you know, the ones killed by Tom Small, Glenda McPhee and Buddy Dickson. Okay, yes, I was there and so I guess in the final analysis or whatever I might be guilty of these people being dead too. But Tom and Glenda and Buddy were the ones who actually did it. They're the ones with the blood on their hands, not me. I'm clean. Clean as a cucumber. Clean as a whistle. I didn't do a goddamn thing, no matter what anyone says. All I did was get them dressed up and set them in motion. They did all the rest. Arrest them if you have a problem. Put them on trial if you can catch them. Execute them all at once—ha!—if you think that's humanly possible.

No, all that guilt and shame nonsense wasn't what was bothering me. It was Buddy Dickson. He was starting to snarl at me. He was starting to chew on those ropes I had tied him up in. No, not real ropes, dummy—like imaginary ropes, metaphorical ones, the big heavy-duty ropes that I had bound him up in after he had gone and killed Rita White. Well, Buddy Dickson had had enough of confinement, thank you very much. He was beginning to whisper in one ear and howl in the other, doing his best to get me to commute his sentence and emancipate his ass. And Buddy, being Buddy, was very persistent about this. He was bullying me, calling me a wimp and a sissy, swearing at me and daring me to be righteous and brave and noble and liberate him from the cell to which he had been exiled. At first, I paid no attention. In fact, I didn't even hear it, this crying of Buddy's for his release. But he grew more and more shrill, and after a while I not only heard his complaint, it was the only thing I could hear. He was not only rattling his chains, he was shaking his shackles and kicking in his stall.

What could I do? I either had to kill him outright or let him loose. And since killing him would involve killing me, that didn't seem like an option. Suicide, at least at that particular point in time, was not even a remote possibility, let alone a viable choice. So I decided to let him loose. Only this time I wouldn't allow him to get out of control. I would keep him on a tight leash. No more flagrant flirtations with Beverly Hills waitresses, no more moonlit escapades up to Mulholland Drive. No more stabs of the knife into the ribs of innocent girls.

When I got Buddy back on, he looked real good and he felt right. I had had to start completely from scratch, as I had burned all his stuff after the incident with Rita White, so I got new duds and a new toupee which fit real snug and looked a lot better than the other one I had used for Buddy.

Buddy and me decided something simple was in order, so we walked up to this Mexican restaurant on Pico and got enchiladas. Buddy was very polite, even with the waitress whose English was pretty rudimentary. On the way home, Buddy said hello to a teenage kid going by on his skateboard and the kid said hi back and I really felt like Buddy was just a regular guy even if he did talk with that vaguely gangsterish-type accent and even though he loved fucking broads and driving Caddies and playing blackjack and betting on the nags. I kept Buddy on when I got home and he and I watched the Lakers play the Cavs. Buddy was really more of a football guy, but being that it was basketball and not football season, he had to settle for this. And he appreciated it, even if it wasn't really his game. Me, I never watched sports, never have, but Buddy of course knew all about that world, the stats, the argot, who was up, who was down, the "skinny" on all the wagers, the odds for this, the odds for that, all that kind of stuff. The Cavs crushed the Lakers and Buddy said that LeBron was a bum and then we got up and went into the kitchen and had a drink.

I didn't have any scotch or any bourbon, Buddy's number one and number two drinks, but I did have some vodka, which Buddy said would do in a pinch, and so he had some straight, of course. Man, Buddy could really hold his liquor! Within an hour, he had downed the whole bottle and we were out the door again. I was really drunk, wasted out of my mind, but Buddy was fine and he walked up the street, no problem, straight and steady as a tree. Me, I was wobbling all over the place, twisting and turning like crazy, but Buddy took me by the arm and led me along like he was rooted to his feet and his feet were sure.

It was maybe eleven o'clock at night, a Thursday as I recall, and Buddy decided we should go downtown to a place called The Perch. So we caught the 733, then we walked to 4th and took the elevator up to The Perch, a place I would never go, as it's way too sophisticated and cool for me, but which of course fit Buddy like the proverbial glove. The view from up there is terrific, downtown spread out below in all its splendor. And the people all look beautiful, young hip types, real pretty girls and guys with cool hats and shades. Me and Buddy, we were easily the oldest folks there, but Buddy Dickson didn't give a shit although I felt kinda strange, like I was intruding in someone else's party. But every party was Buddy's party, as far as he was concerned. And certainly none of these ladies were too young for him. In fact, he was too hot to handle for most of them, or at least that's the way Buddy had it figured. 'Cause right away Buddy started smiling and winking at all the girls, especially the super hot ones, the ones with lots of cleavage showing and long shiny legs as well. Buddy didn't even care if they were with other guys or if those guys saw what he was doing. He actually seemed to like it if these guys shot him a dirty look, you know, like it was a challenge, a challenge to see if he could peel these women away from their men and get them drooling in his lap. In short, Buddy Dickson was a real dawg and I didn't know what the hell to do with him, tear him away and send him home or let him loose for the kill.

Meanwhile, we had a couple of shots of whiskey with beer chasers and boy oh boy, was I drunk! All of downtown L.A. seemed to be reeling beneath me and my feet seemed to be unhinged from my legs while my head was soaring way out over Pershing Square, doing loop-de-loops and nose-diving down to the ground only to flip up at the last possible moment and buzz away into the blue. I thought I might have to go into the men's room and puke, but Buddy held me steady. Man, he could

the briefest of moments, it left this aftermath of bright joy. I had never seen a smile quite like it and neither had Buddy. Buddy figured the smile was just for him, signed, sealed, and delivered, and why shouldn't he have felt that way, given that no one else was around and apparently he was unaware of my existence, at least as far as I could tell.

"Can we just forego the usual crap and cut to the chase," Amy said. She let the smile loose again, and again it flashed so brightly. Okay, so maybe she had had a few teeth whitening jobs and maybe they were caps, for all I knew, but plenty of dames ("dames"? There was Buddy's influence on me) had done the same in this town and they didn't have a smile like hers. "You wanna come to my place or should I come to yours?"

Whereas most guys would've whooped and hollered at this, especially considering Amy's nice big boobs, Buddy groaned like he was real disappointed, like Amy had given him a bad piece of news. "You're destroying the romance of the thing, girl. The hunt, the back-and-forth of the thing, the innuendo, the hints, the whole thing."

"Oh, why bother," she said. "Everyone's a grown-up here. Why not just get down to brass tacks?"

Buddy leaned back on his stool and regarded this woman, like he was sizing her up for something, like she was a mare or a cow or something. Then he said, sort of softly and almost to himself, "Yeah yeah, now I can see it…" And then he nodded his head, as if he had arrived at a conclusion after a long and drawn-out series of thoughts. "I was all wrong…"

"Wrong about what?" Amy was leaning back on her stool now too, like she was mirroring Buddy's action, like me and Buddy were setting up a model and she was following it. "What are you talking about?"

"I'm talking about you and your whole lousy approach to the

romantic interlude. No style to it, no grace. Probably fuck like a dead cow lying out in a field, the mosquitoes all dancing around, the flies starting to bomb-dive and buzz."

She leaned back and laughed at that, breaking the mirroring thing in two, shattering it. "Then you'd be my perfect mate. How old are you, Buddy—sixty? Sixty-five? Seventy?" Then she leaned back into Buddy and me and kind of whispered: "And is your name really Buddy? Why not Max? Or maybe Clyde or something just as old-fashioned and fucked-up as that?"

Buddy laughed, immediately and kind of loudly, loud enough that a couple of people turned and looked at us. "Well, what the fuck do you think my name is, Amy: Rudolf? Amos? Andy? Leroy? Rufus? Fuckhead? Dickwad? Cunt-hair?" As he called off these names, Buddy's voice grew louder and louder, so by the time he got to "Dickwad" and "Cunt-hair" everyone in The Perch was staring and the bartender was moving over to us and fast. He pointed a finger at Buddy and said, "Out of here. Now. Or I call the cops."

"No need to call the cops," Buddy said, smiling. "I am Buddy Dickson. I know when I am not wanted."

"Yeah, well," said the bartender, "then get Buddy Dickson the fuck out of here."

I tried to intervene and apologize but Buddy Dickson wasn't interested in saying sorry, so what difference did it make. "Goodbye, smut hound," he said to Amy as we brushed by her, heading for the elevator.

"Go back to Vegas, you prick," she replied.

On the elevator down, I didn't even know what to say to Buddy. He was such an idiot. And not such a smooth operator either, after everything was said and done. But Buddy didn't care what I thought. He was sticking to his story and following his own path, a different drummer rapping out a staccato-type rhythm inside his head.

Once we got out on the street, Buddy Dickson put his hand in his right coat pocket and felt the hard piece of metal there. What the fuck!?? What was this thing? It felt like—no, it couldn't be—but yes, it most certainly was—a knife! What the hell was this knife doing in Buddy Dickson's pocket? 'Cause I sure as shit hadn't put it there. And the only other person who could have done such a thing was Buddy and he and I had never been apart, as far as I knew, so how had he done this without me knowing anything about it? It was a mystery to me, but now the main thing was not so much how Buddy had got ahold of this knife, but making sure he didn't use it on anybody.

Crossing Fourth Street and heading into the Metro station with those stupid pastel columns of Pershing Square looming up in front of us and the handsome façade of the Biltmore Hotel standing behind them, Buddy swung his hand back around behind him and felt the gun stuck in his waistband. What the hell was this? Since when did Buddy Dickson have a gun? Shit, I must have really fucked up somewhere along the way. A knife? A gun? I had absolutely no memory of getting these weapons for Buddy Dickson and he sure had no business possessing them. But how could I take them away? Buddy Dickson is a lot stronger than I am and he's been in about a million fights and killed one person that I know of, though he's probably killed a whole lot more than that, plus like he's easily the most aggressive person I've ever met, so how could I disarm him or even attempt to disarm him, with such a disparity between us?

The only thing I could do was watch him closely and try and make sure nothing happened. I had to be super vigilant and not let myself slip too much into Buddy Dickson's brain because that brain could go and do anything, fuck the consequences and screw the ramifications and to hell with the mayhem that may follow fast upon his actions. The only hope I had was to get Buddy home safe and sound and then put him away forever and never go back on that decision.

But it turned out Buddy Dickson wasn't ready to go home yet, no matter how hard I tugged at him, and so we veered away from the entrance to the Metro station and headed east on Fourth Street, Buddy Dickson gripping the knife that was pressed tight to his upper thigh. What was Buddy looking for? Did he just want to lash out at someone, anyone, and cut them in two? Did he want to pull out his gun and just go on a spree, killing people right and left until he was mowed down in a hail of gunfire delivered by the LAPD? Or did he just like the feel of the blade against his leg, the way it suddenly gleamed here and there when we passed under a light, the illumination from the metal bouncing off the walls and scattering down the street?

It was maybe one in the morning by this time and the only people in the streets were the crazed and the drunk and the drugged, that and a few of the young hip techies, cell phones strapped to their ears and designer hats on their heads. Buddy Dickson and me were like sore thumbs sticking out of the sidewalk. I felt like neon spotlights were shining on us, lighting up every step we took down the grimy streets. Certainly the police would soon arrive, picking us up just for being here, let alone for carrying a gun and flashing a knife, the existence of both of which I had only just discovered.

But any innocence on my part would surely be offset by the guilt on the part of Buddy Dickson. I had to do something, fast. So with all my might, I shoved Buddy Dickson into an alley. He flailed around and tried to blast me with a right hook, but I ducked and pushed him into a trio of garbage cans overspilling with the reek of the day's remains. Buddy tumbled up right away and struck a fighter's stance but I hit him in his soft spot. That's right, I ripped off his toupee with one decisive swoop, the rug peeling straight off his head and sending Buddy Dickson into a pained crouch, his hand dropping the knife and soaring up to his skull in disbelief. `Fucking goddamn it!' he screeched. I saw my chance and grabbed the blade off the pavement. Then I turned around and threw it as far as I could. The light from the blade switched off and on as it sailed through the air. I couldn't waste any time as I had to get the gun as well.

But when I looked down, Buddy had the gun in his hand and he was pointing it right at my heart. I was looking straight at death and I didn't know what to do.

"You can't get away with this, motherfucker," Buddy growled, and then I said right back at him, "Buddy, don't do it. You kill me and you're going down too," to which Buddy Dickson snorted out a laugh and said, "I don't need you, you piece of shit wimp big pussy asshole," and then I replied with a sense of calm which fell upon me seemingly out of nowhere, "Buddy, believe me. You don't want to kill me. You kill me and you'll never see yourself again."

Buddy snorted again and answered by saying, "Think it's the other way around, schmoe. I take you down and the only thing that's gone is you. I'll still be standing up strong, big dick strapped on, ready to go."

Buddy Dickson was a lot stronger than me and a lot faster too. Plus he'd been in about a billion fights whereas I'd never been in any. So I figured the best thing for me to do was to hightail it out of there, as quickly as I could. This option seemed the only option left anyway, especially when I saw Buddy take that gun out of his waistband and aim it at me. I reached forward and managed to hit Buddy on the wrist as he pulled the trigger. The shot went wild, ricocheting off a dumpster and then smashing through a nearby window, glass shattering down. In the distance, I could hear a siren and I knew it was coming for me and Buddy so I started running as fast as I possibly could, tossing away the gun as I did so. At the end of the alley, right near Fifth and Spring, I twisted out of Buddy's jacket and his shirt and threw them to the ground. Then I tried to act real natural, walking at a normal-like speed as if nothing unusual had happened in like a thousand and one years. I was trying real hard just to be me, Lloyd Stollman, good citizen, even though I still had Buddy's pants on and his shoes too. So I kind of felt like I was ripped right in half, everything on the top being me, Lloyd Stollman, nondescript ex-employee of the DMV, and everything below being Buddy Dickson, Las Vegas card sharp, brute, lover, killer, maniac. This split was very confusing of course, 'cause Buddy Dickson wanted to kill Lloyd Stollman and Lloyd Stollman wanted to obliterate Buddy Dickson, but they were basically stuck with each other, at least for now. I knew that if I could make it home in one piece I could rip off Buddy's shoes and tear off his pants and then not only burn them but burn their ashes as well.

I got on the 33 at Seventh and Main after waiting there in a nervous heap for at least half an hour. No one else was on the bus, not at this hour, thank god. A couple of Mexicans got on at Fig and Venice, two guys who looked like they were pretty fresh over the border and had been out hustling manual labor all day long and most of the night as well.

Though the bus ride was pretty quiet and relatively uneventful, Buddy Dickson wasn't going down easy, that's for sure. He still had his pants on and those sharp-looking shoes as well, all polished up and shiny. At one point, right around Vermont, Buddy stood up and it looked like he was going to head down the aisle, looking for trouble with absolutely anyone, although there was no one on the bus but the driver and the two Mexican laborers, who were drifting off to sleep.

I shouted at Buddy, telling him to sit the fuck down and shut the fuck up. The driver glanced back in his mirror as I shoved Buddy Dickson back down in my seat, but the driver didn't do anything else. After all, it was just some more nuts on the bus at two o'clock in the morning, big fucking deal. The Mexicans didn't even stir, that's how tired they were.

I sat down with Buddy and gave him a good talking-to, telling him he had caused enough trouble for one night, thank you very much, and I had no intention of letting him loose again. Buddy did his usual number, calling me a wimp and a sissy and a faggot and a motherfucking asshole and a whole lot more as well, but his voice was losing steam and mine was getting stronger and stronger. It was almost like I had taken some of Buddy Dickson's power and stuck it into my veins. It was really a lot like life itself was seeping out of him and spilling down onto the dirty greasy floor of the bus and then it was jumping up into me, like the air was going right out of his lungs and he was dying while I was being born.

But I should have known better. Buddy Dickson wasn't dead. Not by a long shot. Buddy Dickson was eternal. Buddy Dickson was like the genie in the bottle. Once he was out, he was out and there was nothing anyone could do. So when I got off at Gramercy and walked up to my house on the sixteen hundred block of Wilton Place, Buddy was still there, walking right beside me, his pants and his shoes still alive with his power.

18

I really needed a break after all those struggles with Buddy Dickson, so I just laid low for a few weeks, only going out to get groceries and stuff. I did a little work around the house, replacing a shade that was busted and touching up some paint in the kitchen. I was thinking of giving up the entire enterprise, retiring all my characters and just living a quiet-type life again. Boring had begun to look good, especially when compared with killing people and waving guns and knives around in the middle of the street.

Plus, I still couldn't figure out how Buddy Dickson had even gotten that knife and that gun. I had no memory of getting them and I wasn't about to try Buddy Dickson on to see if he could remember where he had picked them up, that's for sure. He probably knew, but most likely wouldn't tell me, as he didn't trust me anymore. At least that's how I had it figured.

But one day I was just sitting there watching TV, I don't even remember what it was I was watching, *Comedy Central* or *Breaking Bad* or something, when Fred suddenly came into my head. Remember Fred? The waiter up at the Mexican restaurant near the Blue Whale in West Hollywood. I had met him when I was Benny Monger, gay individual. Gay seemed safe somehow. As if gay people wouldn't go around senselessly killing people. Like they were too sensitive for that. At least that's what I thought at the time.

And besides, like I said, I couldn't get that Fred guy out of my head. There was something about him, not that I was attracted to him or anything, at least I didn't think so, but there was this sweetness about him or a mystery, or maybe a mysterious sweetness or a sweet mysteriousness, something along those lines, that was drawing me to him like he was some sort of magnet or something. It was like Fred lived in a different world and I wanted to visit that other world, explore its surfaces, smell it, see what was what when I got there.

It wasn't about him being a man and me being a man. At least I didn't think so at the time. I had never had any experiences with men. Well, that wasn't quite true, as I had jerked off a guy in high school underneath the football bleachers. His name was Ted Donaldson and it was after school one day and we had been horsing around on the football field, pretending we were professional football players making touchdowns with two seconds left in the Super Bowl, that kind of stuff. Then he'd led me underneath the bleachers, into the slotted shadows with the seats up above. It was like an underground world down there, all subterranean and everything. We sat down next to each other and didn't say anything. There was something magical about it, like we had entered a secret domain. Then after maybe five minutes of total silence, everything real still, he takes my hand and puts it on his dick. It's real hard there, bulging out of his pants. I said something like "What are you doing?" and then he said something like "It's all right, don't worry," and then he zipped down his fly and before I knew it, I was stroking on this thing and he was groaning like some dying baby. It didn't take long for him to come, it happened real fast. And then he just zipped up his pants and we got out of there. Never said anything about it or did it again.

Weird.

Anyway, that was the extent of my sexual experience with males. And like I said, when I was first prepping Benny Monger

I'd actually tried to jerk off thinking about guys but nothing happened. Not even a semi. So it didn't seem like sex was my goal when I got dressed up like Benny Monger again and took off for West Hollywood and that Mexican place near the Blue Whale and that waiter whose name was Fred.

I tried to act gay on the bus but I didn't really know what that meant. Did it mean I should act like Liberace or something? Like I should let my wrists go limp, and lisp when I talk? That was stupid, just a stereotype, and I certainly didn't settle for stereotypes when I got into a disguise. At least I tried not to. First I decided to just be like me except maybe a little more feminine. But that didn't really work as I started feeling too much like Glenda McPhee and the last thing I wanted was for my characters to bump into one another. I went over Benny Monger's biography once again: born in Cleveland, Benny was an only child, his dad a civil engineer and his mom an American housewife. Benny Monger was a great student in high school, almost a prodigy, or so some thought, but then in college at the University of Chicago he had had a breakdown which led to his declaration of homosexuality and his abrupt move to West Hollywood. After that, the bio got a little hazy and I had a sudden queasy feeling, like maybe I should work on it some more before taking Benny out. But then, just as suddenly, I decided to relax and let Benny Monger take over. That was the ticket. Benny eased into my skin and I began to feel him in my guts as he led me into his world. And the first thing that popped into my head was Fred the waiter.

But when I got to the restaurant, there was no Fred. I was kind of shocked, but of course I shouldn't've been: why should he automatically be there? Maybe it was his day off. Maybe he'd been fired or maybe he had quit. Or maybe he was sick. I tried to work up the courage to ask about Fred, maybe my waiter or the maitre d' would know something. But even if they did know something, why would they tell me. Privacy issues and stuff like that, right? But then maybe they would, as it would just be an innocent inquiry. So finally I asked my waiter where was Fred. He smiled kind of like we were teenagers in high school gossiping about so-and-so and I think I might've even blushed. Anyway I got hot and I could feel the crimson stuff run up into my cheeks so hard it felt like my eyes were blushing, if such a thing is possible. My waiter, perhaps realizing that he may have made me feel uncomfortable and not wanting to do such a thing to a customer, dropped the smile and said in a low, confidential tone: "I think he's just running late. He should be here any minute."

Now I was the one smiling, a big sloppy grin I couldn't've suppressed even if I had wanted to, which wasn't the case 'cause I was truly happy. Fred would be arriving soon and I wanted the whole world to know it. This should have been a clue right off the bat, but I didn't recognize it. If I had, I could have prevented a lot of stuff that happened later on down the line. But if anyone's totally capable of navigating the straits of life and never crashing into anything, I sure would like to meet them.

"Coffee?" my waiter asked, and I think there was kind of a smirk on his face because of course he knew I wanted coffee as it would give me the perfect prop with which to while away the time until Fred's arrival. So "Yes," I replied, "coffee would be great."

I didn't have to nudge it along for too long before Fred came in, looking a little hung over or sick or something. But he still looked handsome and nice. Sort of Mexican looking, but maybe Armenian or Persian or something. He went back into the kitchen without glancing at me and that was kind of disappointing. Somehow I thought he would notice me, maybe even come right over and say hello, like we were best buddies or something. I had to remember that I had only been there once before and just because we had exchanged pleasantries and I had left a pretty good tip, that didn't mean he'd be making a beeline for me as soon as were in the same room again. So I just sipped a little more on my cup of coffee and bided my time, trying to act real nonchalant like I wasn't waiting for anything and could care less about what happened about anything.

Of course inside of himself Benny Monger felt a little different, like he couldn't wait to get one more glimpse of Fred and he was dying to chat him up and maybe make some type of play. I was a little surprised at Benny's rising sense of anticipation, his sense of excitement, his general condition of tingling all over. I mean sure, I should have expected this because Benny Monger is gay but I, Lloyd Stollman, am not, so what was going on? It actually took a conscious effort to remember that I was in Benny Monger's body and that this was happening to him and not me. In fact, I should have been happy with what was happening to Benny because all it meant was that me and Benny Monger were doing a real good job melding together. Still, it was a bit much, this twittery thrill with which Benny Monger was waiting, like Fred's appearance would set off sparklers and cherry bombs or something.

Finally, after about ten hours, or so it seemed to Benny Monger, Fred strolled onto the floor in his cute little waiter's outfit, a red shirt, a green bow-tie, black pants and black shoes, Mexican colors. Amazingly, the first thing he did was smile at me and head right to my table.

"Where have you been?" he asked with a flirtatious and devilish little grin.

"Out and about," I answered, trying to be cool when everything inside me was shooting off fireworks.

"I bet you have," he answered, the devilish grin going even broader so that it looked like it might break his face in two. "Can I get you a refill?"

"I need a lot more than a refill." I couldn't believe what Benny Monger was saying. He was proving to be a gay version of Buddy Dickson, at least in the flirtation department.

Fred actually blushed. That was so cute! Look at that, would you! Face going all crimson like a big red pepper. "Wow, you don't mess around," he finally said, and it began to dawn on me and Benny that maybe I had gone too far and needed to rein it in a little bit. But the words out of my mouth didn't reflect that: "Why mess around when you know what you want."

Jesus Christ! What was I getting myself into? But that cute grin of Fred's calmed me down, made me realize that I was going in the right direction, come what may.

Fred bent down a little bit and shifted his voice into a whisper: "Come back at ten," he suggested. "We'll go get a drink."

I gazed up at him and down-shifted the volume and tone of my voice so it matched his: "We better get more than a drink."

Fred leaned back and laughed. "You are too much!"

I laughed too, "You better believe I'm too much."

Fred glanced around. The maitre d' was looking his way. "Gotta get back to work. See you at ten."

19

I'd never been fucked in the ass before and I really didn't understand how I'd gotten here. I mean I guess I understood how Benny Monger got here cause this was something he did all the time, right? But why had I come along for the ride? I was straight, and like I told you, I had only had that one homosexual experience, wanking a guy off underneath the football bleachers in high school, and I'm not sure if that can even be counted as a real homosexual experience 'cause it was more like a teenage prank thing than anything else. But now here I was with Benny Monger in Fred's apartment on Cheremoya Avenue up in Beachwood Canyon and my oh my my asshole was wide open, taking in this guy's big dick until I thought I'd explode. It was weird 'cause it kind of fucking hurt but it kind of fucking felt great at one and the same time. Sort of like Fred's big dick and my wide-open asshole had kind of moved pain and pleasure right next to each other and there they were, combining together and creating something new out of that combination.

Fred's real name was Federico and he was from El Salvador, but his mother was a Russian Jew and only his dad was Salvadoran: that's why I hadn't been able to pinpoint his ethnicity. That was something I was usually pretty good at, spotting ethnic backgrounds and all that, being that I had spent twenty-five years taking snapshots of all sorts of people with all sorts of backgrounds and all shades of skin complexions when I was working for the DMV in Culver City. Federico had come up to the USA a few years ago with his mother, with a coyote charging them three thousand dollars apiece to guide them through the tunnels underneath the border, running from *la migra,* wandering the streets of L.A. until they found a vacant garage in Pico Union. But his mother had died, Fred thinking that all the change was too much for her, and he had lost touch with his dad, who was still down in San Salvador, or at least that's where Fred thought he was. So Fred was a busboy at the Mexican joint for three years and then when his English had improved and he had worn off the hard-edged corners of the newly-arrived immigrant, they moved him up to waiter and he told me all this over wine at La Poubelle down on Franklin before we went up to his apartment on Cheremoya and he ended up putting his dick in my ass.

Now he wasn't talking at all, Federico, now he was just groaning and moaning, well maybe a few words were coming out of his mouth, but they were in Spanish so I didn't understand them and neither did Benny Monger, and anyway Benny Monger was groaning and moaning too, and pretty loudly at that, so me and Benny, we could barely hear anything else except all this groaning and moaning, let alone words, let alone words delivered in a language he and I did not understand, Spanish, that is, *español.*

Now I really started to feel like my asshole might be ripped apart, like right in two, as Federico was driving in there with his cock, like really hard, and I think he was about to reach climax pretty soon. At least Benny and me were hoping that this was the case, as we weren't sure how much more of this we could take, especially me, being that I was new to all this. Finally, this last gasping wrenching sound came out of Fred and I felt him buckling up inside me and then I felt something entering me and I was guessing this was semen shooting inside me and I had to admit that wearing all these disguises and everything had certainly sent me into a lot of new adventures, like who would have ever thought that I, Lloyd Stollman, would end up getting fucked in the ass in an apartment up on Cheremoya by a guy from San Salvador.

Wow! Weird.

I didn't quite know what to think. On the one hand, Benny Monger was pretty damn happy, the fuck in the ass being a thing he always enjoyed, especially when delivered by a handsome young waiter from San Salvador. Me, on the other hand, I was pretty upset, first because my butt hurt like hell but also because I guess I still have leftover moral scruples from childhood or something. Like this was bad or sinful or something. Or did this mean I was really gay and that I would never go see Ting at Touch of Asia again? I wasn't sure…

After the love-making session, Federico and Benny Monger and I took a shower together and I kind of wanted to go home but Benny Monger he wanted to stay, he was happy, like really happy, and he just wanted to stay where we were, horsing around with Federico in the shower and lathering each other up and making silly jokes that were kind of dumb and kind of crude and then afterwards sitting around with just towels wrapped around us and having a nightcap and outside you could hear an owl hooting and then far off up in the canyon a coyote howled and it was all very romantic, at least as far as Benny Monger and Federico were concerned.

Me, I wanted to get out of there. As quickly as possible. First off, my asshole really hurt and I think I even saw some blood seeping out of it in the shower and disappearing down into the drain. I hadn't said anything 'cause Benny Monger and Federico were having such a good old rollicking time and I didn't want to upset them. But now I could hardly sit down, it hurt so bad, and I just wanted to get out of there and give my asshole a rest.

But Benny Monger had a much different idea. He and

Federico were kissing and their tongues were sticking into each other's mouths and it looked like they might just get back in bed and start all over again 'cause now they were kind of groping at each other's privates and Federico's was starting to get hard and Benny had a semi despite what I was feeling. And so they went from the couch to the bed and their towels were falling off their bodies and finally I had just had enough and so I stood up and shouted: "No!"

Federico was like really shocked and stood there agape, his towel around his ankles and his penis abruptly deflating but still holding to a semi position. "What's wrong, Benny?"

"I need to get Benny home, right away."

Federico's face kind of went startled, like he couldn't quite comprehend what Benny Monger was saying about Benny Monger. Or why the hell Benny Monger was talking about Benny Monger in the third person. But I understood. It was crystal clear to me. So Federico said, "What?" like he was attempting to comprehend what was going on and I said "Benny Monger has to get home," and he asked, "And why does Benny Monger have to get home?" and I said, "'Cause Benny Monger's asshole really hurts, for one thing," and then Federico laughed and said, "All the guys say that," and then he reached out while still laughing and tried to grab me and then I don't know what happened but the next thing I saw was Federico's face with his skull busted in and this candlestick all bloody, lying there in front of his nose.

Shit.

A coyote howled and I got Benny Monger dressed as quickly as possible and I made a half-hearted attempt to wipe any prints away with my bloody towel and then I got out of there, holding the towel in my arms.

But before I left, Benny Monger couldn't help himself: he kneeled next to Federico and looked at the cracked skull and the blood running away from it, some of it dripping onto the floor, and the little piece of bone he could see peeking out from the torn scalp and the strange suggestion of a smile which was still lingering there on Federico's face. Death was so still and so silent, Benny couldn't move. I finally had to tear him out of there and get him away from the bleeding skull.

It was maybe three in the morning and I wasn't sure how the hell I was going to get home. Did the bus even run at this time? What about a taxi, that is, if I could find one at this hour? Walking, it would take two or three hours and that was way out of the question. Plus my butt really hurt and I could only move like a bowlegged sailor or something. Then I remembered my cell phone, a device I hardly ever use and I called up Uber and got someone to come right away.

Wow, being up in one of the Hollywood canyons, three in the morning, coyotes howling and owls hooting, branches of trees shifting around in the slow breeze, and right after the person you're with (in this case, Benny Monger) has just bludgeoned someone to death is a mighty strange thing. On the one hand, it felt so right, like wasn't Beachwood Canyon a perfect place for a murder? and it fit in so nicely with the weird tingling strangeness of the Hollywood night. On the other hand, I couldn't have felt worse, a sense of desperation creeping up over every corpuscle of my body.

Most of all, I was disappointed in Benny Monger. I thought he'd be able to handle a real live encounter with another gay person, but evidently he wasn't quite ready for that. For what had he gone and done? He had bashed in Federico's Jewish-Salvadoran head, that's what he had gone and done. I would have to put him under wraps, just like I had with Buddy Dickson. Still, right now, I was in his clothes and I would have to be Benny Monger for a little while longer, at least as long as the ride home.

The Uber driver was Chinese. This kind of surprised me as I had this notion (mistaken, obviously) that all Uber drivers were young white guys fresh out of college who were actually computer-tech geniuses and were driving Uber just until they got their start-up off the ground and made their first billion. But here was this Chinese guy, about my age, and his name was Ho Lee, according to the ID on the dashboard. As we drove down to Franklin and took a left and then a right on Arlington, Ho Lee kept glancing at me as if something was wrong or amiss. Finally, he said, "You all right?" and I replied, "Of course I'm all right, why wouldn't I be all right?" but actually his question made me feel real paranoid, like maybe Federico's blood was smeared across my forehead or something. and then he said, "Towel," and I repeated that one word, "Towel?" and he said "All bloody." He made a vague gesture, indicating the general vicinity of my mid-section. "Towel all bloody."

I looked down and gasped, like audibly. Shit. The towel with Federico's blood smeared all over it was lying there in my lap. "Accident?" the Uber driver suggested.

"Yes, accident. I was trying to call for a driver and I fell over." Oh my god, that sounded incredibly dumb. How do you fall over calling a cab? "Maybe too much to drink," I added, as if that would explain everything.

And it seemed to work: the driver broke into a grin, as if he knew all about what alcohol could do. `Drinking no good. Makes everything fall over and get bloody.' He laughed and I laughed along with him. We were like partners in laughter.

The rest of the ride went without a hitch except that I had the driver drop me off about a block from my house—just in case. Benny Monger gave the driver a really good tip, like a twenty for a ride that cost less than that. But Benny was hoping that the tip might help the Chinese driver forget everything he had seen that night in his car.

Benny Monger and I walked the block to my house and right away we went into the kitchen to burn the towel. It was four in the morning and there were no sounds anywhere, just that crisp noise of something going up in flames and falling apart into ashes. I drank a beer and watched the last of Federico's blood swirl down the drain.

Then I got into bed, but I couldn't go to sleep. Benny was still with me even though I had taken off all his clothes and put him away. But Benny refused to fade away. He kept seeing the bloody tear on Federico's skull and the piece of bone poking through the scalp. Benny Monger felt bad about it all. But there was nothing he could do about it now. So he just looked at the ceiling, wishing he could go back in time. Finally, though, I couldn't stand it anymore, so I turned on my side and tried to go to sleep. But my asshole was so sore from Federico's dick pounding in there that I couldn't get comfortable. Finally, I took three Advil and drifted off, taking Benny Monger along with me.

20

When I woke up it was like three in the afternoon and I was wondering who I was. There was this brief clear moment when I didn't remember anything and then Federico's bloody skull broke into focus and I remembered everything, only I couldn't figure out if it was me or Benny Monger that had taken that candlestick and whacked it across Federico's head. I really wanted to blame Federico, like he had been asking for it and why did he have to go and want more sex when we had already had our fill. But then I knew that Federico wasn't the one who had picked up the candlestick, and Federico wasn't the one who had bashed the candlestick against his skull.

So that left Benny Monger and me. But how could Benny have done this? Benny was gay and he was perfectly willing to have more sex with Federico even though his asshole was bleeding a little. I mean there were other things they could've done and Benny Monger wasn't averse to doing any of them, as long as they gave his asshole a rest. Hadn't Benny Monger actually been sashaying into Federico's arms when the candlestick had suddenly risen into the air and come crashing down onto Federico's skull, opening the scalp and letting out all that blood? So it couldn't have been him.

That left me, Lloyd Stollman. But how could it be me when I wasn't even there? Well, okay, I was there, but only in an indirect way. Like I was there watching everything from way up above, but I wasn't actually involved. I was kind of hovering above the scene, but I wasn't actually in the scene, if you know what I mean.

Heck, I wasn't even gay, so how would I end up in a gay guy's apartment, getting fucked bloody in the ass way past midnight? That doesn't even make sense.

Besides, from what I had seen from my fly-on-the-wall perspective, there had been a big blank space between Federico making a move for more sex to the point in time when the blood from his head began to drip out onto the floor. Anything could have happened in that blank space. Someone else may have come into the apartment. Or Federico may have actually inflicted the blow on his own skull. I know, far-fetched, but it's possible. Or maybe it had been Benny Monger. Or maybe even me. But the point is that no one knows because it's a blank spot, and everything in it seems to have disappeared.

Still, even with that explanation in hand, I felt really bad. There was this nagging sense that I was responsible. In fact, the more I thought about it, the more responsible I felt. I never should have gone out as Benny Monger. I just didn't understand him well enough. There was something smudgy about him from the get-go and it was out of that smudge that the murder had occurred.

There, I said it, okay? The murder. Of course it was a murder. A man's head had been bashed in by a candlestick. A cut had opened up across his skull and blood had dripped onto the carpet. And I was there. I mean Benny Monger was there too, but so was I, Lloyd Stollman. I could have stopped it. I think. I could have run out of the apartment before anything had happened. But then Benny would have been there by himself. And who knows what he would have done? He might have killed Federico and then gone and killed himself as well and then where would I be? Dead, that's what, and that certainly wouldn't've solved anything.

I decided I couldn't think my way out of this muddy situation so I figured it best just to retire into obscurity for a while. I hardly went out, I had my food delivered, and when I did go out it was at night and just to walk around the neighborhood for a little while.

I have to admit, I was getting discouraged with my whole project. Things kept ending up in murder. No one was safe when I put on a disguise. Or at least it seemed that way. And I couldn't just let other people take all the blame. Sure, Buddy Dickson was kind of a psychopath, but I was the one who created him and let him loose on the street. Glenda McPhee and Tom Small had only killed in self-defense: they had solid excuses. And the situation with Benny Monger was inconclusive, the smudgy quality of it making it impossible to figure out, at least for me and Benny Monger. So, really, there was only one murder that I felt was actually my fault: Rita White's. Still, I had done my best to get Buddy Dickson out of there, but he was so much stronger than me that there wasn't much I could do. So maybe I wasn't really responsible for that one, either.

But there was something else lurking inside me as well. And this was hard to admit and it still is hard to admit even to this very day. And that's that there was something I liked about murder. Watching someone go from a live state to a dead state was an unforgettable experience. You can condemn me if you want to, but until you do it yourself, I say you don't know what you're talking about. It really is a thrill. Take my word for it.

Even so, I needed a rest. And I was glad for the vacation from the disguises. Life sort of returned to normal and I even started going out in the day just as myself. I went to a matinee at the Arclight in Hollywood and went back to LACMA to see an exhibition featuring some Gauguins and a couple of Picassos. No one looked at me weird. But I mean of course, why would they? I was just Lloyd Stollman, anonymous, ex-DMV worker, a faceless face in the faceless crowd. Even the police ignored me. One day I walked right past one on Wilshire Boulevard near Arlington and he didn't bat an eye. I guess I fooled him.

One pretty scary thing happened though. The news reported on Federico's death. I saw it in the California Section of the L.A. Times, just a little filler item on page three. But there it was, the identifying features: Beachwood Canyon, head bashed in, the name: Federico Ascuela, age 27. And that's how I learned how old Federico was and that's how I got his last name. But they didn't seem to have any leads, or at least they didn't mention any if they did. So it seemed like Benny Monger was safe, at least for now. And if Benny Monger was safe, then so was I. Right?

Lying in bed one morning, I kept staring at Charley McCoy's Stetson perched there on top of the dresser. Charley had always been good to me. He had never gotten in trouble. Okay, sure, there was that dumb thing on Hollywood Boulevard when he had told those tourists his name was Josh Hawley, but that was before he even knew what his real name was, so that doesn't really count, as how could he know his real name before he knew it?

Slowly and almost ceremoniously, I got Charley McCoy on and man oh man, I felt good in those duds. That was home, old Charley McCoy and the buttes and the prairies and Steve McQueen and Clint Eastwood and Eli Wallach and Scott Brady and William Holden and John Wayne riding right by his side, what a posse! I walked out the door with a big old Western smile on my face, the kind of smile that matches the color and warmth of the sun, the kind of smile that's there for everybody and anybody, old ladies and broken-down ponies and little kids running along in the dust. But nary for a badman. Let a badman be idiot enough to step out of the shadows and Charley McCoy would gun him down without a second thought. That badman would go kerplunk in the dust faster than a turd squeezed out of a goat's ass plops onto the ground, that's how fast that villain would go down.

I could take Charley anywhere too. I knew he wouldn't mess

up. I decided that Silver Lake would be a good destination, so me and Charley took the Western express up to Sunset and then transferred over to the Sunset bus. Nothing much happened but Charley McCoy got a kick out of the ride anyway. He loved all these new-fangled contraptions like buses and cell phones and traffic signals and laptops and all the rest of it too. He wasn't one of those cowpokes who yearned for the past when the plains were empty and the Indians wild and sarsaparilla cost a plugged nickel. The cowpoke lived on, no nostalgia allowed, and he was right at home in the great big middle of the city, for being a cowboy didn't depend on wearing a holster and a Colt .45 and riding all day on a roan stallion without seeing hide nor hair of another person. Being a cowboy was more a frame of mind and Charley and me were snug nestled into that frame of mind, even if we were on an MTA bus headed for Silver Lake.

I got off on Lucille and started walking east. Mostly young folks were out on the streets, the guys with scrubby little goatees and cool hats, the girls with bleached hair and the kind of skirts that were so short they almost didn't seem to have a purpose or function at all. Some of these "hip" folks nodded howdy but most of them didn't bother; they all seemed like they were working hard to give the impression that they were very busy doing creative things and innovating something or other. And that was okay, that's what young folks did: Charley McCoy didn't mind. Charley McCoy used to be young himself and he was still young at heart, a horny colt bucking in the corral, that was Charley McCoy.

Me and Charley felt like it was our purpose to spread good cheer and merry tidings wherever we roamed. It was almost like we were a version of Santa Claus, but instead of a big bag of presents to give away we just had friendly Western-type smiles and howdies for everyone all around. And people responded.

Some of them with just a nod, others with a big "Howdy" right back at us. One girl with a pierced nose and blue-streaked hair even winked at us. Charley McCoy wanted to follow that up and chase it down, but I felt it better that we just keep on straight ahead, heading east to Echo Park.

It was a hot day and I could feel a sheen of sweat on my back. That made me feel good, like I was out on the south forty rounding up cattle. Of course I knew we weren't really out on a ranch, but the feel of the sweat made me and Charley McCoy feel good nevertheless, as if we could have been out on the range, rounding up steers and heifers, galloping down strays and bringing them back into the fold. Maybe me and Charley would head out to Bakersfield some day or Lone Pine or Bishop. Some place where cowboys still ride the range. Some place where a cowpoke can still earn an honest dollar, sleep in a bunkhouse, and get his hands all callused from twirling lariats. Of course I'd have to learn how to ride a horse if I was going to do that, but that would be no problem, as Charley McCoy is bow-legged, account of all the miles he's put on a horse. He can teach me, no problem. Matter of fact, maybe I could just learn by osmosis, Charley just inserting horse-riding knowledge into my bones right through his bones. After all, me and Charley are one and the same, so that kind of thing should be no problem, right?

I crossed Rampart and headed into Echo Park. I reckoned I'd walk up to Alvarado and then catch the bus back home, so I still had a mile or so. Plenty of time for adventure. But not too much adventure, please. I'd had enough of that for a while, what with Benny Monger and Federico and the whole candlestick thing. I still wasn't sure who was responsible for that whole fiasco, me or Benny Monger or Federico or maybe just fate or destiny or something. But Charley McCoy just chalked it up to adventure. This is the West, after all, and stuff happens. Showdowns and ambushes, rustling and hangings, blind men getting blasted in the eyes, Indians scalping poor innocent babes, gay guys getting bludgeoned to death in their Hollywood apartments, it was all one and the same. Did Gary Cooper deserve what came his way in *High Noon*? I don't think so. How about that poor reb played by Elisha Cook Jr. who gets gunned down in the dirt by Jack Palance in *Shane*? That wasn't fair either. Things happened out here in The West and it was just a mystery as to how or why they happened the way they did. A real man had to accept it, adjust, move on. What else could he do? Sit in a corner and cry? Slink into the nearest police station and confess? Jump a ship to Singapore? None of these would do. Best to just walk on, moving up the hill now past Benton Way.

Besides, Charley McCoy didn't have nothing to do with this mess. Charley was clean, his conscience was clear. Charley McCoy had been in a drawer when Federico Ascuela had gotten his brains bashed in, so why should Charley McCoy suffer the consequences? Besides, it was a beautiful day, a little muggy, true, but the southern California sunshine was still beaming down, landing right on Charley McCoy's long lean body as he walked up the sidewalk like a vision out of the Badlands, the buttes and the gullies and the cricks and the plateaus and the arroyos all tucked neat into his brain, all locked steady into the rhythm of his gait.

Me and Charley were so happy, I started humming a song, you know that one about the place where the deer and the antelope roam. Then I actually opened my mouth and started singing the thing, at first kind of quietly and gentle-like, and then I just reckoned what the hell and started belting it out. No one was around anyway, just cars passing by and the occasional bicyclist, so what difference did it make? But shit, I didn't care anyhow. There could have been swarms of people around, I could have been on Fifth Avenue in New York and I still would've belted out the tune, that's how happy me and Charley were, happy enough to be fools, happy enough to be clowns, happy enough to sing at the top of our lungs as we strolled up Sunset Boulevard, bound for Alvarado:

> Oh give me a home where the buffalo roam
> Where the deer and the antelope play
> Where seldom is heard a discouraging word
> And the skies are not cloudy all day!

As we finished off the song, an old Mexican lady passed by with a handcart full of laundry. She had one of those weathered faces that old Mexican ladies sometimes have, ones that look like they have been exposed to decades of raw weather, winds and sunlight teaming up to cut wedges into their skin. She didn't look at me at all, and she didn't glance at Charley either. It was like we didn't exist and that was all right too, as Charley and I were in such a good mood, with the bright southern California sunlight and the singing of the song and all, that nothing and no one could bring us down. So Charley cried out a `Buenas tardes,' to the old lady but she wouldn't be diverted, she just kept walking forward, pushing that cart, head down, eyes on the pavement, her destination the only thing in her mind, or at least that's the way it seemed. Still, the mood Charley and I had created couldn't be busted up by this, the spurning of our offer of good cheer, and so we commenced to whistling a tune as we strolled on up the hill to Alvarado.

When we got there, we were famished and really needed some grub. So we parked our ponies (okay, we didn't have any ponies, but if we had them, we would have tied them up to a pipe or something) and strolled into a diner called The Brite Spot.

We sat at the counter 'cause cowpokes like counters, you're right up next to the action there and you can twirl around on those rotating stools and get a panorama of the whole place if you suspect anything untoward is happening. Plus, your food arrives that much quicker as the waiters and the waitresses don't have to make that long trek to a booth, but can simply shove your plate right across the counter.

Now don't get me wrong, me and Charley appreciated a nice back booth too. One of those plush ones with the fake red leather upholstery that cushions your butt like nobody's business and the curvy shape to them so's you can scoot around and sit here, there and everywhere and slide on out of there whenever you want to, long as no one's blocking the trail. A booth in the back is the spot with the best vantage point as well. So if you're expecting trouble, the back booth is the way to go. But, being as me and Charley weren't expecting any trouble, being as we didn't have an enemy in the world, and being as we were in such good spirits, the stool at the counter was the best bet.

Charley got a hamburger and that meant I had one as well. We both liked everything on it and lots of mustard too, so that's the way we ate it. We ordered a chocolate shake and man oh man, that shake was good! I don't usually indulge myself like this but Charley he reckoned he deserved a shake after all the miles he had put in in the saddle and I had to concur with him: if you've spent most of your adult life (and your childhood and your youth as well, for that matter) on the trail chasing down strays or out on the warpath hunting down Indians or split up into posses galloping after rustlers, killers, and thieves, you'd want a chocolate shake as well and to hell with the calories!

After, we ordered a cup of coffee and that joe was pretty darn good. Me and Charley nursed it along like we had all the time in the world, which is exactly how much we had, in fact. There was no hurry to anything; we could mosey along slow, just watching the slant of the shadows shift around as the sunlight slid around the planet east to west. We also took note of some mighty fine gals, even if their hair was green and purple and blue and their noses and chins pierced and tattoos ran up and down their forearms like cartoons that had escaped from the zoo. One of these gals even went so far as to smile at me and Charley, least I think that's what she was doing, but me and Charley didn't overreact or do anything that a gentleman from Abilene or Tombstone wouldn't do—we just smiled back real polite and tipped our Stetson as a tribute to the lovely lady.

Finally, after about our third refill, we paid our bill and left like a forty percent tip for our waitress and then departed for the bus stop. The ride home was uneventful, just as it was meant to be. I could trust Charley: he was dependable and never wavered from the straight and narrow code of the West. When we got home I was good and tired and I put Charley to sleep, which means that I went to sleep too. As I drifted off, the last thing me and Charley noticed was the Stetson sitting in its place on top of the dresser. Man, that thing was pretty! It was so great being a cowboy. Some day I was going to get a horse.

21

I was so glad to be back on the bus in Glenda McPhee's underwear. Already my cock was bulging up in Glenda's panties and I had to put my purse on my lap just to make sure that no one noticed our erection. It was the 207 Western Avenue bus headed down to South Central and beyond and Glenda and I had no idea where we were going, but we didn't care 'cause we were just in it for the ride anyway and the way the bus vibrated and sent tingles up into our vagina and made our dick hard and rub against our panties. It sure was a thrill and we were so involved we went and closed our eyes and that's something we never should've done 'cause it's a good policy to always be alert on the bus 'cause you never know when trouble might be coming your way and that's exactly what happened, as a teenager looking for trouble sat down next to us, only we didn't know it on account of our eyes being closed and our mind being focused on our vagina and our penis, like I already said.

What got my eyes open was this kid's music. It was blasting so loud it took me right out of the reverie Glenda and I were having, our cock riding up against our underwear, the tip of Glenda's penis going wet against the sheen of her panties, leaving a little damp spot there. So the music was blaring so much it broke my concentration and our erection started to shift down to a semi, and as it did I opened my eyes and looked at this teenager sitting next to me who had his music turned up so loud it could deflate a boner, and did. I glared at this young man—a Latino kid with a Chicago White Sox baseball cap turned around on his head backwards-forwards-like and headphones on and a wife-beater shirt, plain white, but he couldn't notice me or my glare 'cause his eyes were closed and he was rocking his head to his music which was playing so loud it had kicked the props out from underneath my erection.

That's when I decided I should tap this young man on the shoulder. Looking startled, he opened his eyes and looked at me. I said, "Please turn that music down" as politely as I possibly could, given that it had already deflated my penis and disrupted my vagina, but he couldn't hear me due to the fact that he still had his headphones on and his music was still blaring this horrible music which sounded like rap, or maybe it was hip-hop, or maybe a combination of the two, but with Spanish instead of English lyrics and so the whole thing sounded like bastardized mush, just loud horrible bastardized mush, at least in my opinion and that's what Glenda thought too.

Since the young man hadn't made any sort of response I tapped him on the shoulder again but this time he looked straight at me and I noticed that a couple of his teeth were covered in gold and that a thin scar ran across his cheek, pretty much from his left eye all the way down to his neck. This time he took off the headphones, but very slowly and very deliberately, and he seemed to be listening as I said, "Your music. It's too loud. Turn it down. Please."

The kid looked at me for a moment, as if he was having trouble unraveling the fact that there was a person sitting next to him on the bus, let alone what me and Glenda had just said. And indeed that appeared to be the case as he said "What?" exactly as if he had not heard a word I had said. "The music," I said, still trying to maintain at least a veneer of good manners and politeness and respect, and then he said, "What about the music, lady?" and the way he said "lady" was a little ironical or maybe even a lot ironical, and maybe even a little sardonic as well like he knew Glenda wasn't a real lady and he was about to expose her femininity as a façade, or worse. "Could you please turn it down?" I asked, pointing my index finger at the headphones. "It's awfully loud."

He didn't even bother to reply. He just put the headphones back on, closed his eyes again and then actually cranked up the volume a couple of notches. Well, I had a choice. I could either continue with this battle or I could let it go. Or maybe I could change seats and get out of harm's way. Being that I had seen a definite warning on this kid's face, a warning that he might just yank the mask off my disguise and reveal me as a man, and being that he looked like he could tear me apart without too much trouble, being that he was perhaps forty years younger than me, and being that he had that feel of the raw electricity of the streets about him, a familiarity with violence and a readiness to resort to it without a moment's hesitation, I decided my best option was to move to another seat, so I climbed over this kid, who refused to maneuver out of the way, and headed for the back of the bus, which was empty and would therefore be safe. Or so I thought.

I was all at peace, sitting in the back, a good place for the rumble of the big engine of the bus to rev up into your penis and your vagina, and my erection was going good again, good enough so that even though there was no one in the last three rows of the bus and I was really very much alone and isolated there, I still put Glenda's big black purse over my lap, just to make sure no one spotted my big boner covering my vagina.

That's when it happened, that is, I don't know what happened, a car swerving in front of us or something or maybe a pedestrian making a mad dash across the street, but whatever happened, the bus swerved like crazy and everyone on the bus was knocked sideways and jerked around. I fell first to the side and then lurched forward and somehow I ended up flat on my back in the middle of the aisle with my boner sticking up out of Glenda's underwear, a fact which at first I wasn't even aware of, as I was just lying there flat on my back trying to reorient myself and get my bearings back, but a fact I was soon made very aware of as I could hear that same kid's voice, the kid with the headphones and the music turned up way too loud, as he shouted out for all to hear: "Oh my fucking god, would you look at that!"

I lifted up my head and there was the whole busload of passengers staring at me as if they all had one eyeball and were training it together on one spot, my dick, as it flapped up out of Glenda's panties. They were just stunned, struck silent and still, as if the same wave of shock was running through all of them in one seamless pulse. Glenda and me were shocked too, and we were silent and still too as I raced through my mind, trying to come up with an explanation or an excuse, but nothing came up. I mean I couldn't really say something like, "Hi, my name is Lloyd Stollman and I'm a retired DMV worker and this is what I do now for fun, is dress up as different people and roam the city. So, you see, this is Glenda McPhee and she's one of my characters, but yes, that was my cock sticking up out of her panties, so what?" That would never do. So I didn't say anything as my erection tilted down to a semi and I made a move to put it back in Glenda's panties.

"This guy is fucking sick," said the kid, and there seemed to be murmurs of assent to that conclusion all the way around. "Look at him." He pointed at me and started to laugh. "The guy is fucking sick." Everyone else started to laugh too. A toothless old black woman. A white lady carrying a bag of groceries that said "Food 4 Less." A whole family of Mexicans, a mom, a dad, three kids. Even the bus driver, peering at me through the rearview mirror, laughed at the spectacle. "The guy is really fucking sick!"

said the kid for the third time, and now everyone was laughing uproariously, like this was the funniest thing they had ever seen, Glenda and me stuffing our cock back into our panties, getting our wig straightened on our head, brushing the dust off our skirt as we slowly started to rise. "HE IS REALLY FUCKING SICK!"

Where did I get that gun? I mean okay, I reached into Glenda's big black purse and brought it out into the open, pointing it at the kid with the headphones and at everyone else as well, but how in god's name did it get into Glenda's purse in the first place? Of course I didn't have time to answer that question even if I could have, because it, the gun, that is, was in my hand now and I was waving it around at everybody, as Glenda and I shuffled sideways to the door. "Back door!" I cried and the driver opened the door as I moved toward it. Glancing down, I noticed my now flaccid cock was still sticking up out of Glenda's underwear so I stuffed it back in with my left hand while my right hand stayed steady on the gun.

If only that kid had kept quiet. Me and Glenda were nearly gone, the back door open, one leg out of the bus, one leg in when he had to say it one last time: "You are really sick, mister," and then he added that awful line, "You need help."

And so I shot him. Right in the chest. He crumpled, fast, a red mark of blood spreading out from where the bullet went into him. Glenda and I saw this all in one bright flash as we were off and running as fast as we could in those high heels which I still wasn't used to, despite all the practice. I could hear shrieks and shouts behind me and someone crying out, "Call nine-one-one!" and someone else crying "Call the police!"

I took off down a big wide avenue, I think it might have been Vernon, or maybe Slauson, I don't know. Anyway, it was deep in South Central, which meant of course that I would have stood out like a sore thumb even if I had just been Lloyd Stollman, six-foot-two sixty-two-year-old white man, but being that I was Glenda McPhee, six-foot-two sixty-two-year-old white woman, and that me and Glenda were running along super awkwardly in high heels with a gun in our hand, you could say my presence was pretty obvious, to say the least. The first thing I did was get rid of the gun, a gun I didn't even know I had until some three minutes previously. I tossed it into a trashcan and the thing went off when it landed at the bottom of what must have been a nearly empty can. I actually shrieked when it went off, thinking that someone was shooting at me. But I looked over my shoulder and I didn't see anything out of the ordinary: no one running after me, no squad cars descending, no angry murderous crowd swelling up to hunt me down and make a citizen's arrest or something.

But I knew I had to get out of there. So I ducked down a side street and ran about a block and a half till I saw a boarded-up house on the left. Glenda and I figured it was a foreclosure, so we went around back, climbed a fence, picked up a rock, busted a window next to the kitchen door, reached in and unlocked it and entered the house, only to collapse in the middle of the floor, out of breath, shocked and startled by the turn of events—that bullet hole in the middle of the kid's chest, Glenda with the gun in her hand, how had this happened? How had everything gone so terribly awry? We didn't mean to shoot anyone or even hurt anybody, but that kid yelling "HE IS REALLY FUCKING SICK!" and all those other people laughing, and something just snapped and I took the gun out of the purse and then Glenda shot that kid dead and I started running away as fast as I could, taking Glenda with me.

And now here I was in this weird house somewhere deep in South Central, a house going through foreclosure with broken shit all around and cobwebs hanging from the ceiling, and I could hear a helicopter overhead and me and Glenda figured it was the LAPD and we could hear sirens coming in from afar and this looked like the end of Lloyd Stollman's adventures, but just about then I saw the flick of a lighter off to my right and then a sucking sound like someone taking in a big breath, and I was wondering what was going on and Glenda she was real puzzled too and then there was a soft kind of crinkly male voice saying, "Wanna hit, lady?" and I figured why not, what have I got to lose, so this little glass pipe was passed over to me and then I could make out three or four bodies on the floor, all with kind of torn clothes and torn faces as well, and I couldn't tell if they were black people or white people or maybe Mexican or maybe even Asian, it was so dark and shadowy in there, but I was sucking on the pipe by then and the next thing I knew I felt like the top of my skull had sizzled right off my head and a bolt of lightning was hurtling across my brain, illuminating everything, and in that sudden illumination I could see in one blazing picture Buddy Dickson thrusting that knife into Rita White's heart and Tom Small sticking that pen into the Son of Satan's eye and Federico's skull mysteriously cracked in two by the candlestick and the black man strangled in that wedge of dirt underneath the Santa Monica Freeway and then the kid with the headphones shot in the chest with a gun that had appeared out of nowhere and all of it was madness and all of it was insanity and the common denominator was me, Lloyd Stollman, and what the fuck was wrong with me anyway, I had just been trying to have some fun, do something interesting, create a new art form, explore other sides of my being, and now here I was in an abandoned house in the hood, smoking crack, dressed like a woman, five murders on my conscience.

Suddenly I felt ravaged and worn and desolate, and suicide seemed like the only viable option. A huge hole seemed to be opening up inside of me, like a cavern of agony and grief. "Can I have some more?" I asked.

"Just, yeah ... hold on" came a voice out of the jumble of bodies splayed across the floor. And then the glowing pipe came my way again and I lit it up and light flashed and so did my brain. Electric shock hit me again, igniting the inside of my skull, my cranium exploding. Everything suddenly seemed so far removed, I could barely recall my name, let alone that Glenda and I had just shot the headphone kid on the bus. Everything receded, everything faded, me and this light in my head the only things in the universe, glowing together.

And then just as suddenly the light burst and everything compressed together, like everything was collapsing into me, and me and Glenda, our guts were being pressed so tight by some gigantic pneumatic machine or something. Then all the dead bodies came into focus like a gallery of murder being displayed inside my head. Rita White and the blood spurting out of her ribs, the look of absolute disbelief on her face; the black man underneath the freeway, his windpipe breaking (but it was either him or me, and he was trying to cut off Glenda's dick!); the Son of Satan, the pen in his eye; Federico and the candlestick and the blood on the wooden floor of the Cheremoya apartment; and then the headphone kid with HE IS REALLY FUCKING SICK! screaming out of his mouth and all the passengers and even the bus driver laughing. At me. Laughing at me. At me and Glenda. That is, they were laughing until I pulled that gun out of the big black purse and shot the kid down.

That gun… Where had it come from? It had just appeared. As if by magic. But I must have obtained it somewhere. Unless Glenda had gotten it without me knowing. But how could that be?

There was some movement in the corner and some moaning and groaning. It was very hard to see in there, all dark and everything. But as I peered through the darkness, trying to see what was going on, I made out the outline of what I thought were two bodies, their clothes sort of halfway off and they seemed to be rubbing up against one another. I couldn't tell if they were men or women or what, but I decided I needed to get out of there so I started crawling out of the room, aiming for what seemed to be a door. My head was still ricocheting around from the crack I had smoked and so my bearings and my sense of direction were all wobbly and bent out of shape, but I managed to get to the door without straying too far from my course. I reached up and opened the door, leaving the moaning and groaning behind me.

But the new room I entered was even darker and weirder than the one I had just left. Garbage bags were scattered everywhere with piles of unidentifiable stuff tossed here and there. Bodies were lying here and there as well; I could see one woman to my right whose eyes were wide open and I couldn't tell if she was dead or alive, her stare fastened onto the ceiling as if there was some destination up there she was trying desperately to get to, maybe another kind of life was up there or maybe death, but whatever it was, it had her in its grip, her pupils wide and the whites of her eyes gleaming with a feeling I couldn't figure out: maybe hope for death, maybe faith in redemption, maybe nothing and it was all in my mind.

There were piles of clothes tossed here and there on the floor and I began to riffle through them, trying to find something that might fit me and Glenda McPhee. I figured it might be best to get out of Glenda's stuff and try to get back to my house as Lloyd Stollman, anonymous ex-DMV worker who had never committed the mildest infraction against the law, not even jaywalking, let alone murder, let alone five murders. I found some stained blue jeans and a ripped t-shirt and I shimmied out of Glenda's clothes and replaced them with the stuff I had found on the floor. The jeans were too loose by a size or two and the t-shirt too tight by the same but they would do, at least until I got home.

I couldn't figure out what to do with Glenda's clothes. I didn't want to just leave them there; they were evidence, after all, and could be used to chart my escape, if they were found and identified, that is. And I didn't want to bring them with me, as that would even be worse, the evidence right in my arms and difficult to explain if a cop stopped me. What I needed to do was burn them. Just at that moment, as if on cue, a Zippo lighter ignited and a pipe was lit. In the glow I could see a fireplace off to my left. Perfect. I moved forward and grabbed the lighter, which had been deposited on the ground immediately after it had lit the pipe. Once, twice, and then three attempts and finally the lighter ignited and I stuck the flame underneath Glenda's clothes.

The first thing to go was her panties and maybe that's what caused it. The fire, that is. 'Cause I got a little distracted staring at those undies, remembering how my dick had gotten so hard against them when we had rocked and swayed on the bus together. I was getting a rise out of my penis, just thinking about it, maybe a quarter of a dick less than a semi, that is, if you want to measure it, when a spark flew up and landed on a paper bag full of what looked like soiled clothes. And then it just spread so quickly, it was like the whole place was smeared with gasoline just waiting for a match. I only had time to get to the door and get out of there, the fire was picking up speed so fast.

Once outside, I realized I had no shoes, just the pants too loose and the t-shirt too tight. My bare feet hurt like crazy every time they hit the ground and I wished I still had those awful high heels even though they smarted so much and it would've made for a pretty strange outfit what with the pants too loose and the t-shirt too tight and the high heels propping up my ankles all wobbly.

I turned back and looked at the house. Flames were licking at the windows, one man ran out of the front door, screaming, his clothes on fire as he rolled across the dirt in front of the house, trying to put out the flames enveloping his body. I definitely had to get out of there, fast. I turned and ran down the street, glancing up at the street sign as I did so: Budlong Avenue. Somehow that name, just the sound of it, promised bad times, fires, murder, foreclosure, crack cocaine, rape, jaywalking, murder, petty larceny, armed assault, breaking & entering, and the LAPD. I turned off Budlong, if for nothing else than to escape the malevolent aura of that name, its gruesome pall, and ran like hell, screams echoing behind me from the burning house, a siren far off starting to cry, and somewhere even farther off, the rotors of a helicopter.

What should I do? Walk home? Catch the bus? Find another place to hide till morning? Or just find something lethal like a metal spike or something and kill myself? What a mess I had made with my characters! What was that, five, six murders? I couldn't even keep track anymore, that's how bad it was. I should have been content just being Lloyd Stollman. Maybe found a safe hobby like bowling or birding or stamp collecting or something. Or I could have just done some volunteer work, feed the homeless, read to the blind, tutor immigrants in English. But no. I had to invent this new enterprise, the creation of people and taking them out onto the streets for real-life adventures. It had all been too dangerous and unwieldy. It had been one huge mistake.

But it sure had been fun. That is, when it had worked. And it had worked most of the time. At least, that was my estimation. But maybe I wasn't the one who should be doing the estimating, being that here I was, walking barefoot through South Central in pants too loose and t-shirt too tight, it being way past midnight and my mind still glowing with crack cocaine and my conscience trying to navigate through another murder.

Oh well…

I couldn't figure out whether I should run like hell or just walk, try to put on a show of normality, like nothing had happened and nothing ever would. And so I ended up somewhere in between, a kind of halting run or a kind of trotting walk, depending on which end of the telescope you used to look at it. Every streetlight loomed in front of me, their auras of illumination seeming like spotlights, spotlights that were constructed specifically to target me, Lloyd Stollman, AKA Glenda McPhee, AKA Tom Small, AKA Benny Monger, AKA Frank Bunyan, AKA Charlie McCoy, AKA Buddy Dickson. I felt like I wasn't just Lloyd Stollman walking down Normandie Avenue near King Boulevard, but that I was all of my characters simultaneously wrapped into one and that I was wearing all of their clothes, Glenda's high heels, Charlie's Stetson, Tom Small's pocket protector, Buddy's toupee, and Benny's Mephistos. And wearing all those clothes and being all those people at one and the same time made me pretty damn unsteady. I could barely walk, let alone run. At one moment I was using the gait of a cowboy, but then that would be interrupted and Buddy would superimpose his Vegas card shark stance on everything, but then I'd suddenly be wearing high heels, wobbling along, and then Tom Small would take over and I'd be jotting down mental notes about this innovation and that invention. I was getting really confused and disoriented and of course it didn't help that it was way past midnight and I was barefoot in South Central. Plus, I could hear sirens off to the east and I figured they were fire engines headed for the crack house, and maybe cops too, trying to figure out what had happened and what to do.

Just then I got lucky. As I rounded a corner, an idling taxi was sitting right there. I gestured at the driver and for a moment I didn't think he was going to accept me as a customer, what with my bare feet (which I wasn't sure he could see, but which of course I was supremely aware of) and a face which I am positive looked like an alarm bell going off. But then he nodded yes and I got in and gave him my address and before I knew it I was home, safe and sound.

22

Well, I certainly needed a rest after that adventure! And okay, there had been a few mishaps along the way—the kid with the headphones and the bullet in his chest, the crack house and the crack, the fire and then running barefoot through the streets of South Central, Normandie and King, Budlong Avenue and 39th Place, but, when all was said and done, Glenda McPhee had made it home safe and sound and I had made it too.

And then there was that gun. Where the hell had that come from? And it had happened to me twice now, once with Glenda McPhee and the other time with Buddy Dickson. Yet I had no memory of buying one gun, let alone two. Was this just one of those selective memory things, when stuff is omitted from the mind just because it's too weird to keep it in the mind. I had heard about this on Dr. Phil when he interviewed a woman who had driven a car from San Francisco to Omaha to see a dying uncle who had abused her as a child and yet had no recollection of this trip whatsoever. Or maybe it was an onset of early Alzheimer's, stuff erased from the mind just for the erasing. Being that I was just a retired DMV worker, I had no idea what the answer was: that kind of stuff is way beyond my pay grade. Still, it bothered me. I wanted to be in control of the various situations my characters got into and if guns were suddenly popping into my possession without me knowing where the hell they came from, well, that kind of undermined any notion of control, to say the least.

But I had other things to worry about. First, that me and Glenda McPhee and me and Tom Small and me and Buddy Dickson and me and Benny Monger had killed five people, at last count. There was that, with all the moral recriminations and pangs of remorse and guilt by association and just outright personal guilt that that induced. You know, I felt really bad about it. But what could I do? Bring the dead people back to life? I wasn't a magician or a doctor or anything, and I certainly wasn't Jesus Christ. Turn myself in? Oh, I thought about it, believe me. The idea of marching into the police station and confessing didn't bother me all that much. And the idea of prison or even execution, though hardly enticing, wasn't that much of a deterrent either. It was the press, that was the deal-breaker, all the media that would descend on me and turn my life upside down. The photographers shooting photographs of me and the bloggers blogging about me and all that social media stuff, Twitter and Instagram and whatever, and the microphones shoved into my face and the exclusive interview with Diane Sawyer and everything. But it really wasn't my life that I was all that worried about. I could handle it. But Buddy Dickson couldn't take this, and neither could Glenda McPhee or Tom Small or Benny Monger or Charlie McCoy or any of the rest of them. They would be humiliated, shamed, exposed to the nastiest of barbs. And no one would understand their humanity, their beauty, their integrity. Everything I had created would be turned into fodder for titillating sneers and sarcastic jeers. I had to protect every one of my people, and at all costs.

I stayed in for nearly a month. Just had food delivered. Didn't even walk down the block. I sat in the backyard a lot and gazed up at my neighbor's huge sycamore tree. Sometimes, suicidal thoughts floated through my mind. I thought about hopping over the fence and hanging myself from one of the limbs of that tall tree. But that wouldn't be fair to my neighbors, the shock of discovering me hanging from their tree in their backyard, as they had always left me alone, which for me is the ultimate litmus test of being a good neighbor. I thought about cutting my wrists in the bathtub, but then there would be kind of the opposite problem as no one would discover me, maybe for weeks or even months, that is, until the stink of my dead body alerted neighbors and they notified the police. And that didn't seem fair either, as the poor cops coming in would gag the moment they entered the house, a fetid stink coming off my dead body and my flesh all decomposed and crawling with bugs. I also thought a few times about going to the airport and getting on a plane for somewhere, anywhere, it almost didn't matter—Buenos Aires, Tokyo, Paris, Singapore—and just disappearing from sight forever. But I couldn't do that either. I was too set in my ways. I had lived in L.A. for too long. I was old, and trying to change everything around in a foreign country would never work.

So I just had to sit tight and wait this out. I watched a lot of TV, mostly TCM, Robert Osborne, my favorite, he's so urbane and sweet and everything. Plus, he really knows a lot about movies. Which helps. Duh. I especially enjoy the old English movies they show on TCM, you know, like *The Lavender Hill Mob*, *Peeping Tom*, *Brief Encounter*. Boy, the Brits sure know how to make them. And those accents! I sure wish I could talk like that. I tried it out a few times, mimicking Robert Morley in *Beat the Devil*, but it always turned out sounding more like Humphrey Bogart or Peter Lorre than Robert Morley. At least to my ear. I like the noirs too. *No Way Out* and *Pickup on South Street* and *Double Indemnity*, Fred McMurray falling under the fatal charm of Barbara Stanwyck's anklet, that poor schlub, and Edward G. Robinson's little man inside of him that can always tell right from wrong, truth from fib.

Maybe that was what was wrong with me. No little man inside to tell the difference between right and wrong. But no, that wasn't true, as I did know that quite a few things had gone wrong in the course of my adventures. Of course I knew that. After all, five people had been murdered on my watch! I knew I was guilty, all right. But, like I already said, my people shouldn't be punished for my mistakes. It would be like tossing eight or nine people into jail instead of just the one who had committed the crime. It would be like escorting ten or so characters into the gas chamber instead of being satisfied with killing the mastermind, me. That wasn't fair. That wasn't right. That was cruel and unusual punishment of the most dreadful kind.

So, you see, my sense of right and wrong was sharp. It hadn't been eroded by my misadventures. In fact, if anything, it had been heightened. I was differentiating crime and punishment down to the fine details. I was refining the sense of right and wrong into new dimensions. I was setting new standards for morality. I was creating new norms for justice and integrity. And I was doing all that by protecting my people, my characters, my roles, my separated selves who existed in another level of reality, a level of reality that bypassed so-called "normal" rules and codes and regulations. I was operating on multiple levels of reality, seeing things with multiple pairs of eyes, and feeling things that I'm pretty damn sure no one had ever felt before. Given all that, what was I supposed to do? Turn everyone into the cops? Abort the experiment? Give up? I don't think so.

Still…

One day I got out Clarence Finnegan's outfit. You remember Clarence, don't you? Real proper chap, strict morals, a little self-righteous but absolutely fearless, that's Clarence. I put on his seersucker suit, the saddle shoes and the black-rimmed glasses, but I had a hell of a time getting the bow tie on so it looked straight and not like some crazy cattle brand gone awry. Once I had him on, though, he immediately started pacing around the house, denouncing me. He called me a liar and a cheat and a thief and a killer. I tried to remind him that he was as much a part of Lloyd Stollman as any of the other characters, but he wouldn't countenance that. That's how he said it too: "I will not countenance that, you blackguard, you knave." He had grabbed an umbrella for some reason, maybe because it just fit so perfectly with his character, and he repeatedly struck the point of it into the floor as he continued his denunciation. I told him to stop, that I had just had the floors redone about a year ago and I didn't want them punctured and poked and perforated, but he paid no attention and even seemed to strike the point harder into the floor as he went on like a prosecutor trying to convince a jury to give me the death penalty.

I tried to tell him that if I got the death penalty he would get it too, but again he was having none of this, insisting that he, Clarence Finnegan, was beyond reproach and had always obeyed every aspect of the law, right down to its finest nuances and its most refined particulars, so why would the authorities want anything from him? I said that that was all well and good and that I agreed, he had been a very good chap and all of that, but that the law wouldn't see much difference between the two of us when we showed up inside the same body at court. This really seemed to piss Clarence off and he went down the hallway towards my bedroom in a real huff, the hilt of the umbrella moving back and forth in rhythmic syncopation with his gait.

When I caught up with him he was sitting on the bed, staring down at the floor, as if he was lost in deep thought. I sat next to him, waited for a while, giving him time to think through whatever he was thinking through, and then I asked him what was wrong. He sighed, not answering, just continuing to stare down at the floor. Finally he told me that he was keenly disappointed in me, that he had expected a great deal more when he had been recruited into my cast of characters and that he was seriously considering notifying the authorities. I told him that I was pretty darn disappointed in myself too, but that I had thought it through and that I had come to the conclusion that turning everyone into the police would be a horrible mistake, given all the publicity that would certainly ensue, and, moreover, that it would be unfair to subject everyone to that kind of exposure, especially people like him, Clarence Finnegan, who hadn't done anything wrong but would go down with everyone else as if his good behavior and his fine-tuned alignment with codes and regulations had never existed.

Clarence sat for a long time, mulling this over. Finally, he struck the point of the umbrella into the floor, which blow made me wince just a little, given my concern for the floors and all, and then he said that he sympathized with my concerns and he even admired my sense of empathy for all the innocent characters, but that right was right and wrong wrong, and that he would have to march down to the station right now and offer up to the authorities every scrap of information he had. I told him I couldn't allow him to do this, but he insisted, bull-headed do-gooder that he was, and he stood up and started marching to the front door.

That's when I tackled him and wrestled the umbrella out of his hands. I hit him over the head with the umbrella a few times but Clarence was a lot tougher than he looked. Just because he wore a seersucker suit and saddle shoes and a bow tie didn't mean he couldn't take care of himself. Somehow he managed to get away and before I knew it he was out the front door, making a run for it. I caught up with him on the sidewalk and tackled him, both of us crashing to the ground. Clarence bounced right up and so did I and then he assumed the pose of an old-fashioned boxer, both fists up, waving them in little circles in front of his face, like he was following the Marquis of Queensberry Rules or something. I guess he didn't realize that his stance made his middle very vulnerable because I gave him a solid body punch and he doubled over, a huge grunt of pain coming out of him. It sounded weird coming from Clarence who was always so well-mannered and polite. I hesitated for a second, thinking that maybe this body blow would convince him to give up and go back inside.

But at the same time, being that I was both Clarence Finnegan and Lloyd Stollman, I was doubled over with Clarence in pain, and man, that body blow really hurt. But if my opponent thought this would make me surrender, then he had another think a-coming. I straightened up and assumed my position again, fists tucked under my chin, my feet circling, keeping my distance but always staying in range to connect with a hook or a jab.

And Clarence was a lot more clever than I thought he would be, and a lot tougher as well. That body blow sure didn't deter him as he bolted right back into that old-time boxer's stance of his, looking like pictures of John L. Sullivan or Jack Johnson. I decided to dispense with boxing altogether and I turned the confrontation into one of those MMA fights I had seen on TV. I just dove in and tackled him and brought him to the ground and got him in a headlock. I think I actually heard him say "You blackguard," but maybe it was "You bastard," I can't be sure, but what I saw was what concerned me, as out of the corner of my eye I spotted a bunch of people gathering on the street and more than one of them had a cell phone to his ear, and I was certain that 911 and the LAPD were on the other end.

I had to get Clarence out of there as soon as possible and that meant I had to get myself out of there as soon as possible too. So, while Clarence flailed about, moving his arms around in a kind of a speeded-up pinwheel motion, I took him by the scruff of the neck, taking myself by the scruff of the neck as well, and dragged us into the house. I glanced over my shoulder at the threshold and made a quick survey of the scene out on the street.

There were maybe seven or eight or even nine people gathered on the sidewalk with more of them coming out of their houses, wondering what the big fuss was all about. One neighbor, a fat white woman with a gingham dress who looked like something right out of the old Midwest, appeared to be explaining what was going on to a Mexican kid in chinos and a hoodie. She pointed over at me and the kid nodded his head and it almost seemed to me that he was affirming something in his mind that he had suspected all along: the crazy neighbor, that old white guy who lived alone, yeah, he was fucking loco after all, I fucking knew it, Esse. I vaguely recognized these people, but of course I knew none of them, due to my predilection for being alone and not socializing and all.

Slamming the door behind us, Clarence and I leaned up against its inside half and breathed hard. The ruckus had tuckered both of us out and we needed to catch our breath and revive ourselves. Somewhere in the distance I could hear a siren and I suspected it was headed in my direction with backup and maybe a 'copter overhead. I had to get Clarence out of there as quickly as I could so I went to the bedroom and ripped off his clothes. As I stood there in my underwear, I could hear the siren coming closer and a feeling of dread started to move through my guts. But what should I do? Just get dressed up like Lloyd Stollman and pretend that nothing had happened? Run down the street in my underwear, which maybe could be justified as a first step in being labeled a mental incompetent, so that once the sentence came down I would get life in prison rather than the death penalty? Or just stand here in my underwear, waiting for the police to bust down my door?

23

Buddy Dickson was out!

Everybody hear it!

Buddy Dickson was out!

Buddy Dickson had taken over when Lloyd Stollman couldn't figure out what to do. Buddy Dickson knew how to handle a crisis so he shoved Lloyd and everybody else—Charlie McCoy, Glenda McPhee, Tom Small, Clarence Finnegan, Benny Monger and all the rest of them—out of the way and took over. First, he pulled on his clothes and then he went into the bathroom and put the toupee in place. Despite the crisis-like nature of the situation, Buddy smiled at his image in the mirror: it was nice to be back and looking as sharp as ever. Cool as a cucumber, Buddy Dickson made it into the backyard, took the ladder out of the garage, propped it against the back fence, and climbed over it into the back alley.

No one was back there: it was just a long stretch of debris and garbage cans and weirdly assorted remains: a busted-up rocking chair, a couch with its stuffing exploding out of its innards, a slew of metal hangers strewn out on the pavement in what looked like a deliberate pattern, an old pickup truck, and what looked like a ripped-apart section of a blackboard with some algebra equations written on it. Buddy glanced up and down, taking all this in, and then he noted the sound of the siren that seemed to be getting closer every moment.

Buddy knew almost immediately that the pickup was the destination. So he walked calmly, leaning down to pick up a metal hanger on the way. He didn't rush, he certainly didn't run, he just strolled along calmly and coolly, as if it was just another day in the life of and what was there to worry about. After all, he was Buddy Dickson and Buddy Dickson doesn't get flustered or upset or even worried or concerned. Buddy Dickson just rolls with the punches and then strikes back and obliterates his enemy when the right moment arrives. So Buddy Dickson walked up to the pickup, straightening out the hanger as he did so. Then he expertly jimmied open the door with the hanger and Buddy and I climbed into the cab of the truck.

I don't have the faintest clue as to how Buddy Dickson learned how to break into a vehicle because I sure didn't know how to do anything like that, and, being as I am pretty certain I had been with Buddy Dickson during every moment of what could be called his life, and being that I had never received a lesson in breaking into pickups with coat hangers when I was with Buddy Dickson—well, you can understand why I was a little mystified by his expertise and his skills and all. But then we are talking about Buddy Dickson, who is always full of surprises. And, anyway, at the moment I was just thankful that it looked like Buddy Dickson could get us out of there. And I didn't care how he did it, just as long as he did it, and since he was doing it, I had nothing to complain about, I suppose. It was only later that the whole thing went haywire and I regretted everything.

Buddy drove north on Arlington toward the Hollywood Hills. Where he was going, I had no idea: I was just along for the ride, or so it seemed. It was getting on to sunset, the western sky over the Pacific streaked with all sorts of colors, red and orange and, at the horizon, indigo blue and deep purple. Up in the hills, house lights were starting to pop on, thousands of bulbs tracing out electric patterns across the hills, which seemed to be our destination. We crossed Pico and Olympic, Wilshire and Beverly, Melrose and

Santa Monica, and finally Sunset, Hollywood and Franklin. And so I had been right and we were heading into the hills. Buddy Dickson was whistling some tune, some old standard the title of which wouldn't quite come to mind, and the tone of his whistling went in the reverse emotional direction of the crisis I thought we were in, a crisis featuring murders, disguises, and the fight I had gotten into with Clarence Finnegan in my own front yard, the neighbors all around, cell phones in their hands.

Oh well, it had to end sometime. And I had had a great run, taking my characters out on the street and inventing a whole new art form. At least I had done something that people would remember, which is a lot more than can be said for the twenty-five years I had spent at the DMV, snapping people's photos in a cubicle. Sure, maybe it would be a negative-type memory, but at least I would be remembered, that could not be denied. And I was certain that some discerning observers would also be able to see a nobler purpose in my pursuit, an attempt to add something with some zest to life. Sure, there had been a lot of things that had gone wrong, but there were just as many things that had gone right. Think of Charlie McCoy, for instance. Now there was a customer that had never let me down. Always gracious, always kind, always maintaining a good attitude. Plus, he had never killed anyone. At least as far as I knew.

'Cause, see, that was the thing that was really starting to worry me. I couldn't keep track of everything that was happening. You know, like these guns always turning up in people's hands, when I had no idea where the heck they came from. That was troubling. And so maybe it was good that everything was winding down. And, however it ended, it had certainly been an interesting experience. That much could not be denied. And so I was pretty much reconciled with my fate, whatever that would be.

But Buddy Dickson didn't think like that. Buddy Dickson

wasn't reconciled with anything. Things would have to get reconciled with Buddy Dickson and not the other way around. Buddy Dickson was at the wheel and Buddy Dickson was driving. Buddy Dickson was driving the old pickup into the Hollywood Hills, and though I had no idea where Buddy Dickson was going, he sure seemed to have a definite destination in mind, being as he never swerved an inch to the left or the right but just kept that old pickup pointed in the same exact direction, as if something was drawing it on, a gigantic magnet planted in the hills or a woman he had a rendezvous with, waiting for him at the end of the canyons.

Buddy was actually whistling as he and I turned up Beachwood and that was really weird cause I felt like screaming, not whistling, but Buddy Dickson wanted to whistle and so that was what Buddy Dickson was going to do. It was like Buddy Dickson didn't even know how much trouble we were in, what with the fire at the crack house and the fight with Clarence out on the street with all the neighbors watching, not to mention the string of murders trailing after us. Or maybe he knew but just didn't give a shit. To Buddy Dickson, murder was natural, sort of like breathing or playing blackjack or fucking a broad. To Buddy Dickson, fighting somebody else, even if that somebody else happened to be your own self (or at least a version of yourself), out on the streets while the neighbors watched was nothing extraordinary, it was all part of the scenery, kind of like eating a steak or downing a shot of whiskey. To Buddy Dickson, a fire in a crack house or anywhere else, for that matter, was nothing to get all jittery about, he had been through a thousand fires and pulled off dozens of arson jobs, so what. So he was whistling and even smiling and chuckling a little, as if suddenly remembering something that tickled his fancy, like some guy he had coldcocked or some broad he had nailed or some piece of petty larceny he had pulled off.

"You know what I feel like?" he suddenly said, apropos of nothing.

"What?" I asked him, a little wary of the answer.

"A chocolate shake." His smile turned into a grin. "What say you we stop at the Beachwood Café and get us a chocolate shake?"

He wasn't really asking me, like as if he needed or even wanted my permission, so I didn't reply. Buddy Dickson was going to do what Buddy Dickson wanted to do, regardless, so why bother opening my mouth. On the other hand, since I was Buddy Dickson and since that meant that Buddy Dickson was me, maybe I could talk him out of an idea that seemed to be no more than a whim and kinda dangerous anyway, like why put ourselves in the public eye when we didn't need to. "Maybe that's not such a good idea. What with everything that's happened and all."

Buddy Dickson turned and glared at me. "Buddy Dickson wants a chocolate shake. So Buddy Dickson's gonna get a chocolate shake. Savvy?"

I kinda hung my head in shame, kinda like a second grader who's been disciplined by his teacher. "Yeah, okay," I mumbled. "I savvy."

We sat together at a corner table while Buddy Dickson perused the young women in the place, waitresses and customers alike, it didn't matter: he was non-discriminatory, female-wise. The cafe was packed and it was taking forever to get any service and I could tell Buddy was getting antsy so I was getting antsy too. Finally, Buddy grabbed the elbow of a young Mexican busboy passing by, loaded down with dishes. "Hey, Jose," Buddy said, smiling tightly, as if the smile might explode any instant into a roar, "who I gotta fuck to get some service around here."

Buddy Dickson said it loudly enough to make everyone in the place turn and look at him, sitting there with that grin still intact, his hand wrapped around the busboy's elbow. The kid just stared at Buddy. Either he didn't understand a word of English or he was so shocked by Buddy's remark that he couldn't say anything. Regardless, he didn't say anything and Buddy let him go. The busboy headed back to the kitchen and the customers slowly turned away from Buddy and me and went back to their hamburgers and their grilled cheese sandwiches and their Panini wraps or whatever it was they were eating. Buddy sat there, kind of growling and muttering underneath his breath. "Guy just wants a chocolate shake … that's all a guy wants … is that too much for a guy to want …"

I was getting worried. Real worried. Not only was I on the lam in a stolen pickup but I was on the lam in a stolen pickup with Buddy Dickson, a wild card if ever there was one. What the hell were we doing in this place, getting a chocolate shake when we had fled from a fight with Clarence Finnegan and we had five murders on our conscience besides, not to mention the hijacked vehicle? But there was no use trying to reason with Buddy Dickson. Buddy Dickson was beyond logic. Argumentation and reasoning were jokes to Buddy Dickson, crap that only sissies and small-time hoods gave a shit about. He was Buddy Dickson, bulletproof, so far beyond the law that the law did not apply to whatever piece of geography he happened to be in. Buddy Dickson had his own domain that travelled along with him, portable-like, steely, so far beyond rules and regulations that he couldn't recognize or comprehend their meaning.

And that's when he took the pistol out and shot a hole in the ceiling. There were shrieks all around and people ducked and a few fled through the door. `Hey!' Buddy Dickson shouted. "For fuck's sakes—a chocolate shake—to go!"

I tried to get under the table but Buddy Dickson wouldn't let me. He grabbed me by the scruff of the neck and hurled me back in my seat. "Stay right there, Stollman," he growled. "We ain't going nowhere till I get that shake."

The place was absolutely still, absolutely quiet. All heads were turned toward Buddy. The only sound was the shake machine whirring. Apparently, they had gotten the message.

Suddenly, Buddy swiveled and pointed the pistol at a young woman, a redhead wearing a Detroit Tigers baseball cap. "You send that text and I'll blast you, Red," said Buddy, and very convincingly. Then he winked at her lewdly. "Or should I call you 'Tiger'?" The redhead looked at him, completely flabbergasted, and Buddy Dickson turned away from her and took in the crowd. "And that goes for all of you—hands off the phones, motherfuckers!"

I couldn't believe what was happening and I tried to grab the gun but Buddy Dickson wasn't having none of that. He slapped my hand away easily and gave me a glare that would've frozen a wolf in its tracks. "You idiot stupid sissy motherfucker," he hissed at me, "just shut up, sit down and let me handle this." I followed Buddy Dickson's orders and sat there like everyone else, scared as shit, still as could be, not doing a thing to interfere with him and his gun.

The whirring of the shake machine came to a close and I could see the thick brown liquid being poured into a large Styrofoam cup. "Your shake, mister," said a waitress, her voice quivering, "it's all ready."

"Bring it to me, you idiot," Buddy growled. "And two straws. One for me—" and then he gestured at me, which of course meant that he gestured at himself—"and one for my friend."

The waitress followed Buddy Dickson's orders, bringing the shake as she wobbled slowly across the cafe, as if she might faint and fall to the floor at any moment, taking the drink and the straws along with her. She placed the shake on our table as she said very quietly, "Here's your order, sir." Buddy Dickson smiled and said, "Thanks, baby. Maybe if circumstances were different, we coulda—" he smiled lecherously, indicating the "joys" of a sexual encounter with himself, Buddy Dickson. "Sure," she managed, not wanting to do or say anything that might upset this maniac who happened to be sharing a body with me.

Suddenly, a siren could be heard in the distance and this seemed to tickle Buddy Dickson as he smiled and pointed in the general direction of the approaching squad car. "Hey, kids," he said, smiling broadly, "they're playing my song." Then he grabbed hold of the shake and we walked out of the café, Buddy Dickson holding the gun with his right hand and the shake with his left.

"Fuck, coppers!" Buddy Dickson cried as we got out on Beachwood and spotted the squad car coming up the hill. Buddy ducked behind a Prius and took a big gulp out of the chocolate shake. "A little thick," he said, "but I guess she was in a hurry." Then he smiled at me as I was huddling there, literally shaking with fear. "Watch this, Stollman," said Buddy Dickson. "These fucking coppers are gonna get the shock of their lives." Then he handed me the shake. "Leave some for me."

Buddy Dickson came up firing and within five seconds it was over. One of the cops was dead, blasted right in the face, and the other was wounded, rolling on the ground in agony—it looked like his leg, the right one, had taken a bullet, high up the thigh, almost in the groin. I wanted to run over and help the cops, but of course Buddy Dickson was not having any of that as he pushed me into the cab of the truck and off we went, screeching out of there. The wounded cop must have been okay enough to shoot at us because a bullet came through the window of the cab: an inch to the left and it would have wasted me and Buddy. I glanced back as we took off down Beachwood and I could see people swarming out of the café and surrounding the police officers, the one dead, the other wounded.

Well, this was really the end. I could see no way out, but apparently Buddy Dickson did because he was chuckling as he drove the truck down the road like the vehicle was a missile from Hell, gunning it until it seemed like the engine would explode, metal shattering, steering wheel flying off to one side, tires flopping off to the other, seats and upholstery coming undone, stuffing spinning out all over the place, and us passengers landing on our asses in the middle of the street. This was hardly the conclusion I had imagined to my adventure. But what could you expect when Buddy Dickson was in charge?

"Shut up, faggot!" Buddy Dickson growled, even though I hadn't said a thing. I guess he could hear me think. "I'm trying to figure my way out of this mess you've gotten us in," he added, sounding a bit like Ollie from the Laurel and Hardy films.

Now I did say something: "The mess I've gotten us in—you've gotta be crazy. This is your fault, not mine."

"How do you figure that? After all, you're the one got me out of the drawer, not the other way around."

He had a point there. As I tried to come up with an adequate response, I began to hear the sound of something familiar—I glanced up out of the front window: just as I thought, a police helicopter was up there in the sky, following our every move. "You see that?" I asked Buddy as we turned left at Cherokee and wove through the snaking roads of Beachwood Canyon.

"Course I see that." Buddy grinned devilishly. "Nothing that old Buddy Dickson can't outfox." He turned the wheel sharp to the right and I caught a glimpse of the street sign: Cheramoya. This is where Federico lived, the waiter conked over the head with a candlestick by Benny Monger. That night flashed through my head: the rocking motion of our bodies locked together in a wild embrace, the blood dripping out of my ass in the shower, Federico's body lying on the floor, the pool of blood widening out from his head, the candlestick—what a nightmare.

Buddy seemed to know his way through these narrow streets as if by instinct, as if the curving byways had been planned specifically for him. I was suddenly reminded of Matt Damon in the Bourne movies and how he knew the intricacies of every city he landed in, whether it was Moscow or New York or Paris or Tangier. Except that this wasn't a movie, this was real, and Buddy Dickson was neither Jason Bourne nor Matt Damon, he was me and I was him and so we were each other, and we were careening through the roads of the Hollywood Hills, heading over the ridge from Beachwood to Bronson Canyon, pedal to the metal, 'copter overhead, and one dead cop lying in a pool of blood our aftermath.

Fuck! What had I done! Buddy Dickson was out and that meant that Buddy Dickson was in charge and I was just along for the ride, unable to stop this psychopath from wreaking havoc every which way, and of the most vicious kind as well. Oh boy, I wasn't sure how to get out of this one as every time I tried to grab the wheel Buddy gave me a slap in "the puss," as he put it. I think what he really wanted to do was pistol-whip me, but if he had done that he would've pistol-whipped himself, so he passed on that option and just kept fending me off as best as he could. "Leave me alone, faggot!" he cried, slapping me across the kisser as we turned off Graciosa onto Hollyridge.

I got into the corner of the cab and just tried to stay out of Buddy Dickson's way, as there wasn't much I could do anyway, not with Buddy Dickson in charge. Buddy was doing about fifty miles per hour on the narrow streets which couldn't handle more than twenty-five. We scraped against a few walls and at one point sparks burst into the air as the pickup sideswiped a vintage Ford Galaxy, creaming the flanks of the crimson vehicle as we surged by.

Coming down to Franklin, we spotted two squad cars blocking the road at the intersection. Buddy crashed through the blockade, gun blazing, and we tore on out of the Hollywood Hills.

Once past Franklin, the ride turned into a mad dash across the avenues and the boulevards: Hollywood, Sunset, Fountain, Santa Monica, Melrose, Beverly, Wilshire and Olympic as Buddy zigged and zagged the pickup this way and that, always somehow keeping clear of the cops. If it had been me, I would've never made it out of Beachwood Canyon: hell, I never would've made it into Beachwood Canyon. But Buddy Dickson didn't give a shit. Buddy Dickson could haul ass with anyone and do it anywhere. It was like the tires were the palms of Buddy Dickson's hands and he was ripping the rubber right out of them as we descended down the boulevards and the avenues to home. 'Cause that had to be where we were going, right? What else was in this direction? Oh sure, lots of things, an infinite amount of things, in fact. Maybe we were heading for Leimert Park to pay our respects to the homeless black chess players. Maybe it was LAX and a proverbial ticket out of here. Maybe it was the beach and a plunge into the waves, never to come up again.

But was that what Buddy Dickson wanted? Suicide? Nope, not in the usual sense. Buddy Dickson would never give up. A flight from the law? Nope, not that either. He was headed home, no doubt about it, and there he'd barricade himself in and do battle with the cops, to end in a hail of gunfire. Suicide by cop is what folks call it.

Me, so far I was just along for the ride. Hiding in the corner of the cab, wishing me and Buddy Dickson had never crossed paths.

But there he was and so was I. And what could be done?

We roared past Pico and then took a left on Venice. Yeah, we were headed home all right, a helicopter right on our tail. Buddy took a right on Wilton and then swerved the pickup in a wide crazy curve down the half-block to my driveway.

We got out of the pickup firing this way and that, and I fumbled with the keys, of course, but Buddy pushed me aside and got a hold of them and got us into the house. Leaning against the front door from the inside, Buddy let out a sigh of relief and chuckled. "Man, I haven't had this much fun since I killed that bitch up on Mulholland—what the fuck was her name?"

Visions of Rita White danced through my brain and I knew I had to do something, fast. That is, if I was going to protect Glenda and Charlie and everyone else. I tore through my house, flinging off my clothes as I did so and setting the gun down on the dining room table. I could hear a helicopter whirring overhead, multiple sirens descending upon the house from every direction and the sound of a voice coming over one of those metallic p.a. systems: `Step out of your house with your hands up. We have you surrounded.'

I ripped off Buddy Dickson's toupee and stood in my bedroom, dressed only in my underwear. Then I took those off and pulled on a pair of Glenda McPhee's panties.

Again came the command: "We have you surrounded. Come out of the house with your hands up," except this time the words sounded a little more insistent and the tone of the voice more wound up, like words were going to end really soon and action would begin: tear gas projectiles, bullets, the morgue. I pulled on Glenda's clothes as fast as I could and began walking to the front door. But then I remembered the wig. So I returned to the bedroom, grabbed one of the spares and pulled it on tight, checking myself in the mirror to make sure that I looked all right.

Then I took a deep breath and walked to the front door. It felt good to be Glenda, my dick against my panties. Even the high heels weren't too bad, as after all the time with Glenda I had finally kind of mastered them; at least I wasn't falling over with every step I took.

I opened the door. I felt good. I was Glenda McPhee. I was a woman. And the cops wouldn't hurt a woman, would they?

A playwright, poet, actor, and geographer as well as a novelist, Rob Sullivan has written and performed three critically acclaimed solo shows: *Flower Ladies and Pistol Kids, The Long White Dress of Love,* and *Thicker Than Water, Thinner Than Ice.* He was the collaborating writer of *Lady Beth: The Steelworkers' Play,* co-written and performed by steelworkers and staged throughout the United States, including Chicago; Pittsburgh; Asbury Park, New Jersey; Freehold, New Jersey; Washington DC and Manhattan on a tour financed by Bruce Springsteen. He also wrote the play, *The Killing Floor,* for the Hormel slaughterhouse workers of Austin, Minnesota, which was performed in St. Paul, Duluth, Indianapolis and Chicago. Many of Mr. Sullivan's articles and opinion pieces have been published in magazines and newspapers such as *The Village Voice, The Chicago Tribune, Los Angeles Magazine, The San Francisco Chronicle, The Los Angeles Reader, The L.A. Weekly, LIFE Magazine* and *The Los Angeles Times.* Two collections of his poetry have been published, *Wind Rivers* and *Hands in the Stone.* He was a performer with The Mums for over thirty years, acting, juggling and tightrope-walking in three acclaimed shows: *The Death Revue; Mumfukle, or a Small Goat in Crete;* and *MumboJumble,* which Mr. Sullivan co-wrote with Richard Beard and the actor Tim Robbins. He was the playwright for *Rainbow Country,* a collaboration between Montebello Junior High School and the Mark Taper Forum, about immigrants assimilating in America. When he was fifty-three Mr. Sullivan returned to college and earned a PhD in geography at the age of sixty. He has taught geography at Santa Monica College; Cal State University, Northridge; Cal State University, Los Angeles; and UCLA, where he also taught courses in composition. Since receiving his doctorate, Mr. Sullivan has published five scholarly books, including, most recently, *The Metaphysical City: Six Ways of Understanding the Urban Milieu. I, Lloyd Stollman* is his first novel.